"Sir, you can't just—" The nurse visibly fawned as she tried to remain stern, her voice high with excitement and nerves as she continued.

"She knows me." The man stepped into the room, his dark gaze instantly landing on her. "Don't you, Isabel?"

Izzy froze at the sound of her name on Elite One racing legend Grayson Koh's perfectly chiseled lips. For the briefest moment she felt the ridiculous urge to run to him, but then she remembered that while they may technically know one another, they had never been friends.

It had been two years since Grayson had told her she should never have married his best friend, right before he'd offered her money to stay away from the Liang family entirely.

She instantly felt her blood pressure rise.

True to form, Grayson ignored everyone and remained singularly focused upon where she sat frozen on the edge of the exam table.

When he spoke, his voice was a dry rasp. "Am I too late...have you already done it?"

The Fast Track Billionaires' Club

Finding passion at the finish line!

In the elite and glamorous world of motorsport racing, it's not just fast cars that get pulses racing... Especially when three billionaires from the exclusive Falco Racing team come face-to-face with the only women who dare challenge them!

Can former Falco driver Grayson ignore his long-buried desire for the forbidden when he's reunited with his best friend's widow?

Find out in Grayson and Izzy's story

The Bump in Their Forbidden Reunion

Available now!

What will happen when Tristan, notorious playboy owner of Falco Racing, crosses paths with the heiress driving for his rival team?

Find out in Tristan and Nina's story

What will champion driver Apollo do when he discovers the consequence of his passionate night with a beautiful stranger?

Find out in Apollo and Astrid's story

Both coming soon!

Amanda Cinelli

—

THE BUMP IN THEIR FORBIDDEN REUNION

HARLEQUIN
PRESENTS

Recycling programs for this product may not exist in your area.

ISBN-13: 978-1-335-59321-4

The Bump in Their Forbidden Reunion

Copyright © 2024 by Amanda Cinelli

All rights reserved. No part of this book may be used or reproduced in any manner whatsoever without written permission except in the case of brief quotations embodied in critical articles and reviews.

This is a work of fiction. Names, characters, places and incidents are either the product of the author's imagination or are used fictitiously. Any resemblance to actual persons, living or dead, businesses, companies, events or locales is entirely coincidental.

For questions and comments about the quality of this book, please contact us at CustomerService@Harlequin.com.

Harlequin Enterprises ULC
22 Adelaide St. West, 41st Floor
Toronto, Ontario M5H 4E3, Canada
www.Harlequin.com

Printed in U.S.A.

Amanda Cinelli was born into a large Irish Italian family and raised in the leafy-green suburbs of County Dublin, Ireland. After dabbling in a few different career paths, she finally found her calling as an author upon winning an online writing competition with her first finished novel. With three small daughters at home, she usually spends her days doing school runs, changing diapers and writing romance. She still considers herself unbelievably lucky to be able to call this her day job.

Books by Amanda Cinelli

Harlequin Presents

A Ring to Claim Her Crown

Monteverre Marriages

One Night with the Forbidden Princess
Claiming His Replacement Queen

Secret Heirs of Billionaires

The Secret to Marrying Marchesi

The Avelar Family Scandals

The Vows He Must Keep
Returning to Claim His Heir

The Greeks' Race to the Altar

Stolen in Her Wedding Gown
The Billionaire's Last-Minute Marriage
Pregnant in the Italian's Palazzo

Visit the Author Profile page
at Harlequin.com for more titles.

CHAPTER ONE

ISABEL O'SULLIVAN STARED at the chubby-faced babies in the photos that lined the Swiss fertility clinic's testimonial wall and felt her chest tighten with excitement. Today was the day. By this time next year *her* child's picture would be up on this wall too, accompanied by her own smiling face full of maternal joy.

She was finally going to be a mother.

Well, she would be on her way to becoming one if the doctor would hurry back from whatever emergency she'd been called out to.

Izzy had arrived at the glossy marble front desk perfectly on time two hours ago. First they'd struggled to find her charts, and then a series of phone calls had had to be made while she sat out in the waiting room. Now, with every passing minute, she just couldn't shake the feeling that something wasn't quite right.

The clinic was decorated more like a hotel than the plain, sterile hospital where she had done her preliminary check-ups back home, but still she felt nausea threaten, as it did for her in all medical situations. She tried to get comfortable on the examination bed, smiling as her brightly painted toes poked out from the end of the sheet.

A bubble of emotion clogged her throat as she remembered how carefully her best friend Eve had painted the tiny flowers and bumblebees on each toe the night before.

'Because, babe, you're much more terrified of bees than hospitals, so they're bound to cancel each other out.'

Their friendship had once been the closest thing to family that either of them had ever had, after their shared experience of growing up in the Irish foster care system. But Eve had a little family of her own now, with her wife Moira getting ready to give birth to their first child any day.

Izzy was determined to prove that she could do this alone. That she was ready.

A nurse re-entered the room. The same one who had first instructed her to undress an hour ago and then stood completely stone-faced while Izzy awkwardly joked about preferring to be taken out on a date before she got naked. There had even been a loud *tut* when Izzy was taking off her scuffed biker boots, whilst trying to maintain some level of privacy over her plus-sized curves.

She hadn't thought she'd needed to dress for the occasion, but judging by the similar looks that had been thrown her way in the waiting area, her graphic rock band T-shirt and comfy leggings ensemble was a little out of the ordinary from the clothes of their usual clientele.

She had smiled boldly in the other women's direction, resisting the urge to ask if there was·an official dress code for being artificially inseminated with your dead husband's sperm.

After her short-lived marriage to Singaporean playboy Julian Liang she was more than a little familiar with the icy stares that came from not fitting in to the expectations of his social circles. As always, she refused to let it faze her—not when she had managed to make it to Zurich today against all the odds, with Dublin Airport in chaos due to an arctic weather system wreaking havoc across Europe.

But the nurse was not stone-faced now. If anything, she looked a little nervous as she flipped through a chart and looked furtively across to where Izzy quietly swung her legs from her perch on the cold examination table.

She tried not to react when another nurse entered, his face a mask of polite calm even as he leaned in to whisper furiously to his stern-faced colleague. Both shared what Izzy could only describe as *a look*, and began flipping through the forms that Izzy had painstakingly filled out weeks ago online.

She stiffened, her mind expecting a blow even though she knew there weren't any errors. Being dyslexic made written tasks challenging for her, but she knew that she had proofread everything twice with her assistive software.

When Julian had finally confided in her about his possible reproductive issues, after several months of trying for a baby, and had asked her to consider going down the IVF route, she'd thought it wonderful that he was willing to do anything to have a child with her. She'd had no idea that her husband had been freshly out of rehab when he'd eloped with her, and had been using her in a last-ditch attempt to stop his father from cutting him off from his inheritance completely.

Even after she'd found out the truth he'd been filled with promises and pretty words as he'd presented her with plane tickets and the address of a luxury chalet where they would stay during the procedure.

He'd said he was drunk that night he finally admitted the truth, of course. That she was *crazy* to think such a story could ever be true. But for Izzy it had been the first thing he'd ever told her that made complete sense. Suddenly she'd seen the previous year of her marriage for what it was, and walking away had become an act of salvation rather than cowardice.

She wasn't crazy. She never had been.

It had been easy to put the idea of ever having a family of her own out of her head as she'd fought for the courage to begin the process of divorce. But then, before she'd been able to do so, he'd died. His overdose had been ruled as likely accidental, but they would never truly know.

She hadn't loved Julian. Not really. Not the way she'd believed she had when she'd agreed to marry him after only two weeks together. He had been charming, and exciting, and she had been reeling from finding out that her contract as a nanny in a position that had begun to feel like home wasn't being renewed. And, yes, perhaps there had been a little rebellion at play, considering that Julian's egomaniac racing driver best friend had been to blame for her sudden joblessness.

Since dropping out of school at sixteen she'd had all sorts of jobs, from simple waitressing gigs to a wedding singer, and even a face painter in a travelling circus. She had never been able to understand how anyone was happy to pick just one career; she wanted to try all of them. And so she had, accidentally landing her first nannying gig when a wealthy family had spied her face-painting at a kids' party and taken a shine to her.

Moving around the world from family to family had been an exciting way to see the world at first, but soon it had become her normal.

The position with Astrid Lewis, the PR manager for one of the Elite One class racing teams, Falco Roux Motorsport, and her young son Luca had only been meant to be temporary, but she had clicked with little Luca and his powerful single mum, and her two-month contract had turned into an entire year.

Travelling around the world, attending the glamorous motor races and caring for an adorable toddler had been a dream job, but she had got too attached.

Abandonment, even if only perceived, had always been her biggest trigger. It was the lonely, small part of her that still bore wounds from being moved around so often as a child. She closed her eyes, hating the fact that this prolonged waiting period had brought back all these difficult memories on what was supposed to be a wonderful day.

It had been two years since she'd become a widow at twenty-five, and she had spent that time trying to stay in one place for the first time in her life and doing the kind of soul-deep recovery work that she'd always run from.

She'd bought a house. The first one she'd ever had of her own. Sure, it was a rundown little cottage that she'd had to spend the past year renovating with her own two hands, but it was hers, and she paid the mortgage with her book illustration work. She'd always loved drawing and was grateful that she'd found a career in it after Astrid had let her go.

But taking this final gift that Julian had given her—his sperm, still stored at this clinic—was a once-in-a-lifetime opportunity for her to give herself the dream she'd always longed for. She was going to create a little family of her own and, best of all, nobody would be able to take it away from her.

With the warm, invigorating glow of that reminder, she closed her eyes to begin her practised calming regime of inhaling and exhaling in slow sequence. She was supposed to imagine that she was blowing the sounds away with each exhalation and breathing in an oasis of calm with each inhalation…or something like that. But the sound of faraway voices was fast intruding upon her oasis with what sounded like an increasingly fraught argument.

She huffed out a breath, cursing herself for believing that her therapist's deep breathing techniques would work on her deeply ingrained hyper-alert ways.

Another chorus of voices sounded, right outside

the examination room's door now, and Izzy sat up impatiently. Evidently she was cursed when it came to actually getting this treatment today.

'Ms O'Sullivan's is the sole name on this account. We weren't aware that any further action was necessary.'

Izzy felt her entire body deflate. Further action? Had Julian not fully paid off the account? He had always been terrible with money.

She closed her eyes, mentally calculating how much money she had in her savings and hoping that it would be enough to straighten things out. She had only just entered her fertile window, so even if they had to wait for a bank transfer she could arrange to stay in town for a couple more days.

She could come back tomorrow. She could sort this out.

She inhaled another deep breath and prepared to get up—only to find herself frozen in place as a familiar voice sounded out in the hallway, raised above the others.

'Tell me which room she is in. *Now.*'

The icy demand was laced with the kind of cool threat that she had only ever heard from one man before in her life. But there was no way *he* would be here, in Switzerland of all places. You couldn't conjure someone up simply by thinking of them.

She swung her legs over the side of the table, just managing to cover her lower half with the sheet as the door was pushed open.

Her view was mostly obscured, but from what she

could see a handful of clinic staff had formed a con-cerned crowd around a broad-shouldered figure. The sour-faced nurse had moved to stand guard in the doorway, a blush high on her cheeks as she attempted to appear stern and immovable. But just as quickly as she'd begun frowning she looked up—and promptly melted back against the doorframe.

'Sir, you can't just…' The nurse visibly fawned even as she tried to remain stern, her voice high with excitement and nerves as she continued, 'I mean… I'm such a huge fan. But only assigned partners are permitted in this area, or people who are known to the patient.'

'She knows me.'

The man stepped into the room, his dark gaze in-stantly landing on her.

'Don't you, Isabel?'

Izzy froze at the sound of her name on motor rac-ing legend Grayson Koh's perfectly chiselled lips. For the briefest moment she felt a ridiculous urge to run to him—the one familiar face she'd seen since being stuck waiting in this posh, frigid place all morning. But then she remembered that while they might technically know one another, they had never been friends. Even if for a while she'd thought they might be.

It had been two years since they'd stood shoulder to shoulder as Julian's remains were loaded onto the Liang family's private jet. Two years since Grayson had told her she should never have married his best friend in the first place—right before he'd offered her money to stay away from the Liang family entirely.

She instantly felt her blood pressure rise.

True to form, Grayson ignored everyone and remained singularly focused upon where she sat, frozen on the edge of the examination table. His eyes seemed to burn with urgency as he scanned her half-clad form, his eyes coming to rest upon the neat trolley by her side, filled with sterile implements and tubes.

For a man famous for his icy control, on and off the racetrack, his expression flickered with a sudden wildness that she had never seen before.

When he spoke, his voice was a dry rasp, his throat straining as he seemed to struggle to form words. 'Am I too late…have you already done it?'

'That's none of your business.' She subconsciously guarded herself with folded arms, feeling her pulse throb at the base of her throat. 'W-why are you here?'

She hated how weak her voice sounded, with an audience of doctors and nurses watching their little exchange. His shrewd gaze seemed to follow her every move, missing nothing and giving nothing in return. She shivered, feeling thoroughly exposed.

'The insemination.' His eyes narrowed upon her. 'Has it already been done, Isabel?'

She flinched back. Embarrassment and anger began to creep in where her surprise had held her immobile. It was so typical of Grayson Koh to barge into *her* private appointment and make her feel as though *she* was the one who had done something wrong. His look of stern disapproval was one she had become quite used to whenever she'd been visiting the racetrack with his young godson in tow. The fact that she'd had an unbearable crush on him back then was now unthinkable.

'Who do you think you are to barge in here and make demands?' she asked, putting as much steel into her voice as she could muster, considering her entire body had already been under stress and she was close to fainting.

Of all the times that Grayson could have shown up in her life, it had to be today. It had to be here.

She had seen emotion on his face that day in Dublin, when he had appeared in the hospital only hours after Julian's death. He wasn't as ruthless as the media portrayed him. He was simply effortlessly aloof, notorious in his sport for his calm confidence and bravado. He was infinitely sure of himself and his ability as a legend in the world's most fast-paced sport.

He had always looked devilishly handsome in his sleek racing suit and trademark gold helmet, but now…freshly retired and rocking a shirt and formal trousers…he was still the most beautiful person she'd ever seen up close. It was an assault to the senses just looking at him.

The news of his recent retirement had been shocking, and impossible to avoid in the news, but as always she'd forced herself not to think too much about it. Not after the way he'd spoken to her on the day she'd laid her husband—his best friend—to rest.

She had wondered if Grayson blamed her. After

all, if Julian hadn't followed her to Dublin, and insisted upon remaining there while he attempted to woo her back as his wife, maybe he wouldn't have relapsed. But of course no one else knew Julian's secrets.

Perhaps that was why Izzy had given him more chances than she ever would have given anyone else. She had recognised the struggle in him. It had been the same lonely emptiness that she had seen in her friends who hadn't made it very far once they'd all aged out of the foster care system. She'd always had Eve back then, at least.

Grayson stepped through the doorway, closing it behind him. 'You didn't think to consult me before travelling here? Did you really think that I wouldn't find out?' he asked, levelling her with a cool stare.

'Why on earth would I need to consult you?'

She readjusted the sheet on her lap, hardly believing this moment was happening for real. Maybe she had fallen asleep on the examination table and this was all just some weird, very messed-up dream.

'If you're here on behalf of the Liang family, I have already signed every legal waiver known to man. I know full well there will be no inheritance for Julian's child, just as there was none for his widow.'

'*Julian's* child? Why would you think that you were…?' A horrified expression transformed Grayson's handsome features. 'My God. You have no idea, do you?'

'No idea about what, Grayson? You barge in here, to a private examination room, like the hounds of hell are at your feet. And you expect me to simply know what I've done wrong?' She inhaled a sharp breath, needing her worst fears confirmed. 'Did you…did you pay for the treatment on Julian's behalf, or something? Have you rushed here just to make a scene of informing me that I'm in your debt? Or are you here to tell me you won't pay for it at all?'

Grayson cursed under his breath. 'You think that I'd rush out of a meeting in Monaco and break every speed limit to get here over a supposed *debt*? I came here to close the account. To put a stop to it all just as I should have done long before now.'

Cold seeped into Izzy's chest, snuffing out all the hope that had fuelled her through this hellish day so far. What kind of terrible luck had she accrued in her lifetime that the one person standing between her and the only thing she wanted was *him*? In the year she'd spent travelling alongside the Elite One racing teams he'd made it clear how much he disapproved of her with a series of icy stares and cold shoulders. He hadn't deemed her fit to be his godson's nanny, and now he was trying to stand in the way of her having a child of her own.

'You can't do this, Grayson. I'll cover the cost myself somehow,' she said, her voice dripping with a mixture of shock and fury.

But if he stood against it she knew that with his financial power and influence she'd never be able to go ahead. And even if she wanted to pay for it herself, she knew she couldn't afford the entire bill.

He continued to stare daggers at her, his nostrils flaring as though she'd just kicked him in the gut.

'This damned place…the whole agreement…' He cursed, dragging a hand over the light stubble on his sharp jawline. 'All this time…and you didn't even *know*?'

Izzy raised a palm, unable to listen to his imperious tones a moment longer. She was absolutely furious, and so very done with how people seemed intent upon judging her and assuming the worst of her today.

'Oh, I *know*. I know that I've wrestled with this decision for the past two years and that I came here today to carry out Julian's last wish…for me to have a child. Those were the last words he spoke to me the day before he died—other than telling me to call *you*, of all people. You can't just…cancel this, like it's a bank account. Like it's *nothing*.'

The last word came out perilously close to a sob, and Izzy felt the swift scald of tears prickle her eyes.

She bit down hard on her inner cheek, refusing to unravel here, in this place. She just needed him to leave. She needed him to disappear and for everything to go back to the plan that she had so carefully lined up. She'd taken the next week off work. It was a new year. It was a fresh start. She had finally felt fully in control of her path forward—and now here was Grayson, standing in her way.

'It's not nothing to me,' he said, his hard features blazing with some strange emotion as he took a step towards her. 'Isabel, we need to talk—'

'*Get out*!' she said with a growl as she hopped off

the table. 'I don't want to talk to you. You may have the wealth and authority to cancel my plans at will, but this is a private examination room you've just barged into.'

Grayson froze, looking briefly down to where her bare legs and feet poked out from the bottom of the sheet she'd hastily wrapped around her waist.

'Of course,' he said abruptly, turning away from her. 'Take a moment to dress. I'm going to go and speak with the doctor. And then…then we can discuss our situation.'

Had he seriously just referred to this as *their* situation?

She didn't bother to correct him. Didn't bother to say anything else at all. She just pushed him out of the room and closed the door behind him with a snap. Once she was alone, she leaned forward, pressing her forehead against the cold wooden panels.

Her breath came harder.

She looked around at the implements on the trolley and felt the dizziness come closer. She needed fresh air. She needed to get outside…to breathe… Get away from Grayson Koh's dominating presence. Once he was gone, maybe then she would be able to figure this out.

She inhaled another deep breath, trying to ignore the rising panic in her chest as she pulled on her clothes as fast as she could.

Grayson hadn't bothered to wait for the doctor to open her office door, instead storming in and placing his hands down heavily on the woman's desk by way of greeting.

'Mr-Mr Koh…' the doctor stuttered. 'I've been informed of the situation, and I must issue my full apologies. The account has already been nullified and your sample has been sent to be destroyed.'

'Good,' he growled. 'Now I'd like to know how this almost happened in the first place.'

'Well, Ms O' Sullivan had already booked for the insemination before the death of her husband, so it was simply listed as a pause—'

'She doesn't know it's my sample,' Grayson gritted. 'I'm pretty sure that violates something in your damned terms and conditions.'

The doctor sat upright. 'That's impossible. She signed the contracts.'

'It's clear that she doesn't know the sample is mine.'

Grayson emphasised each word through gritted teeth, closing his eyes against the memory of her staring at him in confusion when he'd questioned her decision to come here without his knowledge. He'd assumed her dislike of him was the reason she'd never openly addressed the deal he'd made with Julian, against all his better judgement.

My wife desperately wants a child,' his friend had begged, *'and it's your fault I can't give her one.'*

Even today she had spoken of her plans, her hopes…and he was the villain in her story once again.

Guilt rose in his stomach.

'She thinks she's being inseminated with a donation from her late husband today. Not mine.'

The woman stood up, straightening to her full, impressive height. 'That's a very serious accusation, Mr Koh. We take meticulous measures to ensure that all parties are fully briefed before we carry out treatments involving donors. I can assure you—'

A thought suddenly occurred to Grayson. 'Are they briefed in writing?'

'Well, in this case, yes. Considering she resides in Ireland, today was Ms O'Sullivan's first in-person visit.'

Isabel had never openly discussed her dyslexia, but his young godson had told him about his nanny's fancy phone apps, and upon watching more closely, he'd noticed all the ways she overcame her challenges himself. Not that he'd spent a lot of time watching her, of course. She'd just always seemed to be around during that season. Everywhere he'd turned there she'd been, filling up the space with her laughter and smiles.

The doctor was pacing now, using a sheaf of papers to fan herself, as though she too had just realised how close they had come to having a woman accidentally inseminated by the wrong man.

'Your voicemail this morning simply said we must delay the appointment.' She winced. 'I thought perhaps it was a payment dispute...'

'You are quite aware of my public standing? Do you think that I would simply disclose such sensitive information in an email? No. I've had to drive across Europe in a snowstorm. Praying that I would get here in time because every flight from Monaco was cancelled.'

Every moment of that drive had been agony, and he had arrived to find his friend's widow on an examination table…unknowingly readying herself for a procedure that had the potential to intertwine their lives for ever.

There was a reason why he had told Julian he could no longer give his blessing for his donation mere days after giving it. It had been that moment when he'd first imagined Isabel O'Sullivan pregnant with his child.

Grayson closed his eyes and inhaled a shaky breath, pinching the bridge of his nose. If he'd got here just half an hour later that very well might have been on its way to happening.

The thought struck at something dark and greedy within him. A feeling he'd tried to bury for three years now, since the scandalous elopement that had made Izzy Julian's wife. He'd practically sent her running into his best friend's arms when he'd shattered that careful distance between them with an illicit kiss in his darkened garage, then selfishly asked his friend Astrid not to renew her nanny's contract just so that he could secretly be free to pursue her.

It made sense that she had no clue that Grayson had been a part of this arrangement. He should have known she'd never have agreed to accept such personal, long-lasting help from a man she'd made it clear she would never trust again.

Julian had never shown even the slightest interest

in marriage and children before meeting Isabel, preferring instead to live the life of a playboy bachelor. Grayson had assured Julian that he would never claim paternity of the child. It had been the least he could do after Julian had revealed to him that his infertility was due to the racetrack accident that had left him unable to drive ever again.

They had both been young drivers then, filled with ego and the desire to win a much-coveted seat with an Elite One racing team. But as the son of a housekeeper and a chauffeur, Grayson had needed to toe the line and earn billionaire Peter Liang's patronage to avoid being forced out of the sport entirely. Even if it had meant quite literally driving his best friend off the road.

Grayson closed his eyes at the familiar tightening of emotion in his throat that came whenever he thought of Julian. Their parents had been close friends, despite Grayson's parents being their longtime employees. The Liangs had been kind to him, even paying for him to join Julian at a private school in England, where they had both started their careers on the karting tracks. Of course his relationship with Julian's father was what had driven a wedge between the two friends in the end.

Damn Julian's lies. Damn him. It was unbearably cruel that Isabel had lost her husband in such an abrupt fashion. Had she thought of this child as her last link to him?

'I need you to come with me and explain the situation to her,' Grayson said, straightening to his full height and unbuttoning the top button of his dress shirt.

When he had received his bank's notification that payment for the procedure had been initiated by the clinic, he had raced out of an important meeting about an upcoming charity race in Singapore.

'Of course.' The doctor nervously cleared her throat. 'I just need to assure you that this has never happened before.'

Grayson realised the clinic's employees were likely quaking at the idea of potentially major legal ramifications. But of course he wasn't the party who had been wrongfully treated.

'I will take full responsibility if she wishes to sue, or if she wishes to wring my neck—whatever it takes. I just need you to help me talk to her.'

'Absolutely.' The doctor fanned herself again, her face turning a deep pink hue as she called a nurse in from the hallway. 'Gianni, we will need to get Ms O'Sullivan into one of the nicer consultation rooms.'

The nurse frowned. 'She walked out a short while ago.'

'She…what?' Grayson felt his blood pressure spike.

'She seemed quite upset,' the nurse said quietly. 'She mumbled something about needing some air, but then I heard her car skidding out of the car park.'

'In this weather?' the doctor asked, appalled. 'Conditions mean we're actually closing early for the weekend. The airports and train stations are all closed too. She can't have gone far.'

Grayson cursed under his breath, launching himself out into the hallway and striding towards the exit doors. He had no intention of returning on any other day. And Izzy wouldn't be returning either—not once he'd explained everything to her.

CHAPTER TWO

Izzy FOCUSED ON getting her tiny rental car uphill in the heaviest snowfall she had ever seen.

One call to try to get an earlier flight home had quickly informed her that the airport had grounded all flights for the remainder of the day, due to the severe weather conditions.

Her eyes burned with tears she refused to shed. Crying didn't get anything accomplished when the world pulled the rug out from beneath you—she had learned that pretty fast as a child. She preferred to be practical and focused, pushing through challenging times until she had a solution.

But this… She had no idea how to make it right. She didn't have the kind of money that it would take to foot the bill at the clinic herself, and there was no way she would crawl to Grayson for charity. His loyalties would always be with the powerful Liang family— the people who had refused even to acknowledge her marriage to their son and publicly decried her as an opportunist.

Just a few more miles and she would be at the

address detailed in Julian's letter. The place where she had envisaged herself resting after her successful appointment—not running to in order to nurse the overwhelming waves of disappointment coursing through her.

She bit down on her lower lip until it hurt, refusing to let herself break apart. She just needed to get out of the snow and then she could begin to attempt to unravel the mess of her perfectly laid plans.

Judging by the speed of the growing snowdrifts, she would be staying up here for the night, at least. A prickle of unease slid down her spine as she realised how isolated it was on this winding mountain road. Her car had already slid perilously close to the guardrail a couple of times, despite the well-treated Swiss roads.

The chalet couldn't be much further from here, could it? The map on her phone showed her destination was around the next curve in the mountain, but the road seemed to be rapidly becoming a sharp incline.

When a small lay-by appeared on the curve, she pulled to a safe stop, deciding she would rather walk the next few kilometres safely than continue to risk the drive. She should have stayed below in the town and tried to find a hotel room for the night.

Cursing, she grabbed her small overnight backpack and began trudging uphill, suddenly thankful that she'd thought to wear boots in lieu of canvas sneakers. These were surely waterproof, at least.

Her leather coat did little to protect her neck from

the icy winds, though, and she discovered the hard way that her boots were built more for fashion than functionality. Damp trickles of water soon leaked through to her thin cotton socks, and she was pretty sure if she didn't get indoors soon she'd turn to ice.

By the time she reached the heavy gate at the top of the lane her breath was coming in bursts and she was shivering violently.

In Ireland, a snowstorm like this would shut the entire country down for days—but she'd thought a place like Switzerland would be accustomed to freezing weather conditions.

Finally she spied a sleek white access panel, and hastily pulled out her phone to get the code that would unlock the electronic gate system. After multiple failed attempts, thanks to her overly stressed mind, the system beeped and the gate opened to reveal a stunning chalet crafted in glass and natural wood.

It was split across multiple levels and carved into the face of the mountain. At the moment the snow fully obscured what she would guess was a panorama of spectacular views from the front. Through the hedging on her right she could see steps leading up to the next level, where she possibly might find a front door, but she was freezing, and her thighs burned from the uphill climb.

Had Julian thought that he would bring her here himself? Had he wondered if it might lead to a reconciliation, despite her telling him over and over again that their marriage would never recover from his lies and manipulation?

She pressed the code into another panel on the wall and watched as one of the heavy garage doors slid upwards on invisible hinges. Eager to get out of the snow, she walked inside quickly, groaning in relief at the comparative warmth of the dark basement space. She didn't need to adjust to the darkness for long, as automatic lighting switched on in slow motion, revealing a cavernous workspace that smelled of engine oil and rubber. Rows of cars spread out before her, some of them fully built, while others were suspended and surrounded by high-tech equipment.

She wandered along the rows of vehicles, searching for an exit from the garage, and finally found one towards the end. It required yet another code, of course, because clearly whoever owned this place was obsessed with security.

She was infinitely grateful as she opened the door and felt much warmer air envelop her as she made her way up a staircase.

To call this place a chalet seemed absolutely absurd, for the formal entryway she now stood in was more like the entrance to a boutique hotel than a mountaintop retreat. The entire floor was decorated in warm oak and polished stone, offset with sleek furnishings and textiles that gave hints of burnished gold and strategic accents of red. Her eye was drawn to the stunning glass floor-to-ceiling hearth that dominated the main living space, bracketed by a plush L-shaped red velvet couch.

She roamed the opulent upper floors in a haze of confusion, noting that each bedroom had a four-poster bed larger than any she had ever slept in in her life, and looked out upon spectacular sweeping views of the valley below.

She felt like an intruder, and just being there made her every nerve stand to attention. But it was clear from the storm outside that she would need to stay the night. Despite her misgivings, she forced herself to sit down on the red-cushioned sofa downstairs, and let her head fall back against the plush headrest.

The prospect of being potentially snowed in at a strange place was not a big deal for a girl who had grown up knowing she might be shipped off to another foster home at any given moment. It steeled her, that thought. Reminding her of how she'd forged her way out of the difficult life she'd been told she should expect as the daughter of a troubled teenaged runaway. She'd refused to become another statistic— the victim of a broken system like her beautiful birth mother had been. She was strong. She would not let the events of today throw her.

She was still going to have a child, somehow. She might not know the exact details just yet, but she was not going to allow one man to cow her into giving up.

The image of Grayson towering in the clinic doorway was still burned into her mind. She hadn't seen him once since the day he'd left to accompany Julian's remains to Singapore. She had not been invited to the Liang family's private ceremony there, and he had seemed angry to find out that she didn't intend to fight them and ensure she was adequately settled financially.

She'd been disarmed by his kindness over those two days. He'd even organised for her to stay in his hotel suite in the city while they dealt with the funeral arrangements. She'd been awash with grief and he had been comforting and attentive, ensuring that she ate, and even sleeping on the sofa in her room when she had nightmares.

She hadn't had the energy to feel awkward, even considering the last time they'd seen one another had been the night before she'd left Singapore on Julian's yacht. Neither of them had ever addressed that kiss, but it had remained burned into her memory ever since. Just as the awful day that had followed had too.

After receiving nothing but Grayson's stony silence for the duration of her short marriage, whilst they'd grieved together she'd begun to believe, for a moment, that maybe she'd been wrong about him. Maybe he wasn't the cold, ruthless egomaniac that he was so often portrayed as in the press. In those quiet moments as they'd stood side by side in the crematorium, he'd even held her hand.

Her husband had known that it was Grayson who had first captured her attention when she'd begun attending the Elite One races. He'd known that it was her hurt at learning Grayson had asked Astrid not to renew her contract that had led to her hasty agreement to travel to Bali on Julian's yacht.

She wasn't entirely oblivious to the reasons behind her own actions. She knew that she had some lingering issues with forming secure attachments to people. It had taken Julian's death for her to finally begin doing the necessary work to heal that part of herself—hence why she had got to the point where she finally felt ready and able to move on to the next part of her life. To start a family of her own, nurture her own roots, and settle down for the first time in her life.

Astrid had lost her previous nanny in the midst of the frantic run-up to the new Elite One season. Luca, her two-year-old son, had been obsessed with motor racing, and the godson of legend Grayson Koh. Izzy hadn't known what to expect after essentially joining a group of people who clearly knew each other very well, but everyone had adored Luca, so by extension she was welcomed by the Falco Roux crew with open arms.

Well, most of the Falco Roux crew.

From first glance, Grayson had been cold towards her. His strong personality was a well-known fact, mostly attributed to his preternaturally ferocious drive and talent. It didn't help that he was possibly the most handsome man she had ever set eyes on, and she did nothing but babble nervously in his presence.

He'd seemed to dominate every room he entered, with his shrewd gaze and chiselled jawline, and on the few occasions she had seen him smile her heart had pumped painfully in her chest. Yes, she had developed quite a crush on him over the following months, as she'd spent time in relative proximity to him.

She'd learned quickly that life on the road during the season was hectic and isolating, so the Falco Roux crew treated one another as friends, eating meals together and blowing off steam on their off days.

Grayson had been suspicious of her easy acceptance into the fold, and had even begun to linger around her and Luca in his off time. Astrid had been curious as to why he was calling in to visit his godson more often than he usually did. Izzy had known it was likely that he disliked her wild hair-colour changes and was afraid her free-spirited attitude would ruin his tiny protégé.

Until that kiss.

She was sure that no one knew about the illicit kiss she'd shared with Grayson after the last race of the season, but afterwards, Astrid had begun to behave oddly around her. At the party on their final night in Singapore, before their planned return to London, she'd revealed that she would not be extending Izzy's contract after all.

After that emotional equivalent of a bucket of cold water being thrown over her Izzy had been only vaguely aware of Astrid hugging her, gushing that she had some connections for selling her book illustrations if she was interested. Izzy remembered pasting on a bright smile and flinging herself into enjoying the rest of the party as much as she possibly could.

Copious amounts of alcohol later, she'd found herself being consoled in Julian Liang's arms. He'd been so easy to talk to, so adventurous and free with his compliments and open thoughts.

When Julian had asked her to travel to Bali with him the next day, just as friends, Izzy had jumped at the chance to run away from yet another painful rejection. He had told her everything she wanted to hear—that he had been falling for her over the few times they had met over the previous year, that he had decided he wished to settle down and start a family... and the rest was history.

They had been married a matter of weeks later.

Apparently Grayson had called him a few times, utterly furious. It hadn't been a surprise to Izzy that people had believed *she* was the one taking advantage of charming, fun-loving Julian Liang. And even less of a surprise when no one had believed her when she'd eventually discovered the painful truth behind their sudden elopement.

Julian had been on his way to bankruptcy, and had decided the fastest way to force his wealthy parents to cut him in on his future inheritance was via the promise of grandchildren.

She froze, suddenly processing that she'd been staring up at a large impressionist-style painting of an eerily familiar gold motor racing helmet. The cold efficiency of the layout had set off some hidden warning in the back of her mind that she'd been ignoring before. She stood up, looking around her for something to prove the increasing sense of recognition wrong. But sure enough, the more she actually looked at her surroundings, the more evidence she saw everywhere.

The walls and shelves were mostly bare, except for a glass case that contained a row of golden trophies. She moved closer to look at the inscription on one of the bases and jumped back as though burned.

Julian had sent her to Grayson's home.

After having already hidden from her the fact that he had let Grayson pay for the insemination, Julian had also just handed his friend's private security codes to her.

None of this made sense—but she wouldn't be staying around to find out why he'd done it.

She had just grabbed her bag and run into the foyer when the front door burst inwards. Snow swirled, framing the broad silhouette of the last man she wanted to see.

'How the hell did you get up here?' Grayson growled, his voice a furious echo.

'I walked,' she said, determined not to squirm.

'In a blizzard? Do you have no care for your own safety? When I realised that you'd attempted to drive...' He inhaled sharply, rubbing a hand against his chest. 'You abandoned your car on the side of the road. I thought you had been...'

Izzy looked at him. He thought she had been hurt. His heavy breathing, the frantic look in his eyes... It wasn't anger. It was...concern.

'This was the address in my information pack. I wouldn't have come here if I'd known that this place was yours.' She blurted out the words, moving cagily around him towards the still open door. 'Don't worry. I was just leaving.'

'Don't go.'

She ignored his command, hoisting her bag over

her shoulder and walking out into the icy air. The snow was falling so thickly now it had already formed a fluffy blanket upon the car Grayson had arrived in. It was a heavy-duty SUV—much better to scale the mountain roads than her tiny rental hatchback had been. But driving downhill would be easier, surely?

She had no other choice. Because staying up here alone with him was not an option.

She heard his footsteps crunch through the snow in her wake.

'For God's sake, Isabel, stop running from me. There are things we need to discuss…things I have to explain.'

'I don't need you to explain. You chose to come here and ensure that my appointment was cancelled without even giving me the option to pay the bill myself. What's done cannot be undone. You can just stay up here in your beautiful ice palace,' she called back, trying not to be alarmed at the sound of his heavy steps pounding closer. 'It's perfectly matched with your personality after all.'

Proud of herself for that parting line, she picked up her pace as much as she could manage, trying not to feel alarmed at the depth of the snowbanks that now lined the road. She couldn't have been up here any longer than an hour, and yet the world outside had been transformed from a white wonderland into more of a Snowmageddon situation.

Her senses screamed at her to retreat, to go back inside, but she never had been good at backing down from her own impulsive decisions. It was a double-edged trait. Once she committed, she followed through. Not out of willpower or determination, but out of pure, unfiltered spite.

She had barely left the driveway and had taken no more than a few steps along the downhill slope of the lane when her boots began to lose their grip on the frozen ground. A vision of herself sliding down off the edge of the mountain came into stunning focus in her mind, and the utter foolishness of this endeavour crashed down upon her.

She was fighting to keep her balance, just managing to keep one foot stubbornly in front of the other, when she felt hands clamp down upon her shoulders.

Grayson's face was a mask of tightly controlled irritation as he spun her around to face him.

'Do you despise me so much that you'd risk falling to your death?'

His breath steamed in the frozen air and the heat of his strong hands seemed to scorch her even though she wore three layers. Almost as quickly as he'd grabbed hold of her, he let her go. She swayed a little on her feet, but refused to let him see how unsteady she felt.

It was a bone-deep shakiness that wasn't just because of the weather. She felt…inconvenient. And immature. As if she had been left in the dark about some important fact. She'd thought she had all her plans in order, that she knew exactly what came next, but now it felt as if those plans had been swept out from under her, leaving her adrift and vulnerable. It was a feeling that triggered all her darkest fears.

'I just need to get down to my car,' she said weakly.

'It's likely buried in a snowdrift by now,' he gritted, taking her by the hand and abruptly cursing. 'You're freezing. We need to get back to the house. Let me say what I need to say, and then I'll stay out of your way until the blizzard passes, if that's what you want.'

She debated fighting him, but the snow was still falling in thick blankets—more than she had ever seen in her life. Far from feeling like a winter wonderland, it felt…scary. As if, if she stood still for long enough, it might bury her too.

After a moment's pause she began walking ahead of him back up the steep hill, refusing to take his hand as they trudged towards the chalet.

Once she was standing back in front of the giant fireplace, watching as he set about lighting it and getting them both steaming cups of some kind of herbal tea, she felt panic crawl in her chest.

Until this snow cleared she was trapped here with him.

No place to run.

He stood on the opposite edge of the hearth, stirring his tea slowly, as though he was afraid he might scare her again. As though he had gleaned just how jumpy she was around outward displays of anger… how they made her heart race as if she was a small child all over again.

'I'm going to talk now, and you are going to listen. Understood?'

He took a few deep breaths, looking briefly towards the still-open doorway of the living room that led back to the foyer, but not moving to close it.

'There are things you don't know about the clinic. Things that I assumed Julian had explained to you.'

'Is it about the money to pay for the procedure?' she prompted.

'No. Not about the money.'

Grayson closed his eyes, pinching the bridge of his nose with one hand, and for a moment she thought he looked absolutely tortured—which made no sense. This was a man who did not show weakness or discomfort. Ever. Perfection was his brand, for goodness' sake. And yet right now she could tell that something was very, very wrong.

Her heartbeat drummed loudly in her chest, and she held her breath in her throat as she took a seat back on the red couch. Reflexively she reached out for her tea, cradling it in her hands as though it might provide her with some kind of comfort in the face of whatever terrible secret or new detail this man was about to reveal to her.

So much of her marriage had been built on deception and dishonesty—she honestly didn't know if she could take any more. But if therapy had taught her one thing it was that she was resilient, and that was something to be proud of.

Grayson paced to the window, then back to the open fire. She had seen him like this before, unable to stand still when he was talking. It seemed to impede his focus somehow. Clearly whatever he was about to tell her required his full concentration.

'Isabel, the sample at the clinic…it wasn't Julian's.' Grayson met her gaze. 'If I'd arrived too late today… if you'd already gone through with the insemination and it had resulted in a child…the baby would have been mine.'

CHAPTER THREE

OF ALL THE potential reactions that Grayson had considered while he'd been driving up the mountain, preparing to reveal the truth, he hadn't expected cold indifference.

He had taken a lucky guess that she would seek shelter in his chalet, knowing that had been part of Julian's original plan. Now he inwardly cursed, staring down at the stony-faced woman on his red velvet sofa. Her fresh-faced beauty and luscious curves were still as perfect as ever, but her spirit was dimmed.

The Isabel he'd once known had always been very fast and free in her responses—the first person to laugh or grumble in conversation. But now, instead of shouting at him or bursting into tears, she seemed to be crumbling in upon herself, piece by piece.

She'd made no move to question what he'd told her, so he kept going. He told her about the text Julian had sent to him, asking to meet up. How Julian had told Grayson his marriage was in trouble, because Isabel wanted a child and Julian couldn't give her one because he was infertile. He told her how he,

Grayson, was the reason for that, and so his guilt had led him to agree to be the sperm donor, waiving all rights to paternity.

When she still didn't respond, he opted to give her some space to process everything. He moved away and set about calling various authorities, only to confirm that they were, in fact, snowbound for the foreseeable future. All the main transport links were closed, and people were being urged to stay indoors until tomorrow afternoon at the very earliest.

Isabel, obviously having heard most of this via his side of the aggravated phone conversations, asked which bedroom she could use to rest in, and when he showed her promptly disappeared behind the heavy wooden door with a final-sounding click. He hovered in the hallway, wanting to ensure she was okay, but he also remembered his promise to leave her alone once he'd said what he needed to say.

He'd done that. He'd explained himself... So why didn't he feel any better?

An hour passed and still nothing but silence came from her room, while the snow continued to fall hard and heavy outside.

Usually he paid a management company good money to have his residences ready at all times, as with his international schedule he never quite knew when he might need to stay in any of the properties he owned around the world. But, of course, with the current weather that had not been possible today. Still, the freezer still contained some choice cuts of meat from his last stay, and the larder held a decent assortment of jars and dried foods. He wasn't a chef, by any means, but he could rustle up something decent when needed.

The words seemed to be frozen in his chest as he thought over everything that had been said. The fact that Julian had intended to have Isabel carry another man's child without her knowledge was utterly unconscionable. But the fact that he himself had never even thought to speak with Isabel before agreeing to Julian's request made him complicit as well.

He had simply assumed that it was what Isabel wanted. He had even made sure to have legal documents drawn up that would prevent her from claiming financial benefits from him in the event that her marriage to Julian failed.

The knowledge that all he had considered was the risk to himself shamed him anew.

But the one thing he hadn't considered at all back then was the effect it would have on him once he'd allowed himself to envisage Isabel carrying his child. He had done his very best not to think of it, even in a hypothetical sense. But in the days immediately after he completed his part in the agreement, something had changed.

He had picked up the phone to call Julian numerous times, to tell him everything was off and to risk the friendship that they had rekindled. But every time he'd thought of the words he needed to say to end the deal he'd remembered that he was the reason why Julian was in this position at all.

Julian had told him how badly Isabel wished to

have a child, and how he had initially lied to her about his own infertility, thinking it would stop her from marrying him. He'd said that now they had decided to go ahead with sperm donation they both wished for their donor to be someone they knew.

That had been the story he'd been told. But now, linking together all the small bits of information he'd discovered over the past couple of years about his oldest friend, he didn't know what the truth was any more.

He knew that Isabel was not a fool, but he also knew how manipulative and selfish his friend had been when he was at his worst. Julian had commented on Grayson's behaviour around Isabel more than once, noticing his lack of focus whenever she was with them. He'd known that Julian had been cut off financially from his family, that his addiction was spiralling once again, and he'd refused to lend him any more money, widening the rift between them.

It was his fault that Isabel was in this situation. If anything, he'd wounded her and sent her off into Julian's arms like a perfectly presented gift.

He brooded for the rest of the afternoon and until the late evening, when finally Isabel emerged from her bedroom in search of food. He watched as she gathered up some crackers, then walked over to the windows to stare out mournfully at the conditions outside.

'Can I make you more tea?' His words came out roughly, and snappier than he'd intended, making her brows rise.

He forced what he hoped was a neutral expression to his face, not wanting to continue the frosty silence that had settled between them. They were going to be stuck here for the night, judging by the weather reports, and possibly for the next day also.

'I think the situation calls for a little more than tea, don't you?' she said. Her voice was detached, and still devoid of her usual energy and emotion.

He stood motionless as she made her way over to the ornate drinks cabinet on the opposite side of the room. She ran her fingers over each bottle, lightly tinkling the glass, finally coming to rest upon the neck of a top-shelf whisky. Not the choice he would've imagined for the smiling Irish girl he had only ever seen drink soda with a straw, like a teenager.

She poured herself a generous amount, then tilted her head back and proceeded to down it in one gulp.

'That's not a good idea.' He walked across to her and slid the bottle very firmly away from her reach.

'Give it back,' she said, and there was a little more fire in her tone now.

'Not until we talk this through soberly.'

'What exactly is there to "talk through", Grayson?' Her eyes narrowed on him, and her purple-tipped fingers gripped the crystal glass she held in her hand. 'Would you like to discuss the fact that Julian's lies almost resulted in me unknowingly carrying your baby? Or would you like to discuss the fact that you actually agreed to his mad proposal in the first place?'

'I told you—I agreed to it believing that you knew all about it.'

'And you thought that I wouldn't want to speak to you about it myself? Ask you what your intentions might have been?'

'It's no secret that I caused the accident that led to Julian's early exit from motorsport. But it's not common knowledge that his injuries resulted in him being told he would never father a child. For years I tried to find a way to make it up to him, and he finally came to me and gave me that chance. My part was to stay anonymous.'

'So it was some kind of penance?' She stared at him, her expression filled with ire.

'After I'd agreed I barely lasted a week. I called him the night he died. I called him and told him that I couldn't go through with it. And then he went out and overdosed.'

'All this time…did you think that was why he did it?' She shook her head sadly at Grayson's solemn nod. 'Well, that was the same night I told him I wouldn't go through with it either. So I guess that makes us quite the pair, doesn't it?'

Grief and regret burned shamefully in his throat. He held back the torrent of excuses on the tip of his tongue, the cleverly worded arguments that would extricate him from his guilt. Because as he looked at this strong, beautiful fireball of a woman imploding before his eyes he knew that now was not the time for any of that. Now was the time to remain silent and let her be.

Even if that meant allowing her to reach out and grab the bottle of whisky from his hands.

She filled her glass and then popped earbuds in her ears. He could only vaguely make out the sound of some kind of heavy rock music—her genre of choice, he remembered, along with bubblegum pop and show tunes.

He remembered far too much about this woman for his own comfort.

He watched as she downed another two glasses of his whisky, but thankfully seemed to rethink having a fourth. She kicked off her boots and swayed gently from side to side as the music took hold of her, and he was powerless to look away, telling himself that he remained seated where he was simply to ensure that she didn't get hurt.

She was blowing off some steam and, truthfully, he had nothing else better to do.

He moved away, into his office. He had already gone through his more urgent work emails, and fired off a few of his own relating to the annual charity Legends race, which was being held in his home country of Singapore next month, in honour of him being the latest racing legend to have retired.

It would be the ideal time for him to unveil his business plans going forward, as he moved from being a shareholder in Verdant Race Tech to being its CEO.

Verdant was an exciting sustainable-energy-focused auto engineering firm. He'd been a shareholder since the company's infancy, ten years ago, having seen their potential for innovation across the entire motorsport industry and beyond. His plan was to launch his own team in next year's Elite E—the highly competitive league that used the world's fastest electronically powered cars.

He had also founded the Boost Academy—a global motor racing initiative that provided a springboard for disadvantaged youth.

He hadn't been home much recently, with his work so often taking him around the world. But now, since his retirement, he wouldn't have the same level of engagements from week to week. His restlessness had been one of the factors that had been tempting him to accept one of the countless offers he'd received to return to the sport. To end his career on a high.

The Verdant factory and headquarters were currently set up in Monaco, to capitalise on it being a hotbed of talent for motorsport professionals, but he'd kept his own role remote while he'd been competing.

He had set up the business to be flexible on purpose, after learning the most up to date methods from his successful corporate friends. And over the past two decades, since the very start of his racing career he'd learned what to do and what never to do. He knew better than anyone the corruption and malpractices of the wealthy elite.

He'd kept his lifestyle in check, ensuring that he never lost sight of what his parents had raised him to be, even after they were no longer around to see it. But his ethics and business practices were a separate entity entirely from his image…his persona as racing legend Grayson Koh.

Julian had always called his wife Dizzy—their

little joke, he'd said. It had never felt like a joke to Grayson. He's thought it unnecessary and demeaning to Isabel. But then again everyone said he took things too seriously. He couldn't relax…have some fun.

So Isabel had never truly met the real him—not really. She had only ever seen the driver, the personality that he'd adopted as part of his drive to dominate his sport. It had been a necessary role for him to play, for he had discovered from an early age that when he won, when he performed at his absolute max, he was accepted by everyone—unlike when he'd just been a nerdy kid with working-class parents.

Elite One was an expensive sport, and Julian's father liked winners. So the legend had been born. He'd always had a temper on the track, and the impatience, the cold arrogance he'd shown in interviews, had grown with him as he'd risen up through the various Elite platforms, finally reaching the pinnacle that was Elite One.

When he had been behind the wheel or on the podium he had felt powerful. He hadn't even noticed that the powerful persona he'd adopted had begun to seep into his day-to-day life until eventually he'd rarely let his real self take the reins at all.

A loud splash sounded from the other side of the door, jolting Grayson from his thoughts. He looked down at his watch and realised he had been in his office far longer than he'd intended.

Quickly, he made his way back into the main room—only to find it empty. The doors to the partially covered balcony were spread wide open, letting in the chilly night air, and when he stepped out he was met with the sight of Isabel sliding her partially clothed body into the hot tub.

He reached it just as she submerged herself, up to her waist, and cursed as he saw her shivering violently. Before she had been wearing only a black wool jumper and skinny jeans with rips in the knees—not exactly warm winter attire. But she had since stripped down to a simple black camisole, and he had briefly seen matching black lace-edged panties. Not that he had been looking.

He had long since trained himself to stop looking at Isabel O'Sullivan.

He cleared his throat loudly to announce his arrival, satisfied when she jumped a little and crossed her arms defiantly over her ample chest. She was clearly absolutely freezing, and likely already regretting this ridiculous venture. The covered terrace was purpose-built for the winter months, but even with the heated tiles and steaming water the air was still cold if one was not fully submerged. Most of all, she was very clearly drunk. This was a most unsafe activity.

'Don't be a spoilsport,' she said, pushing his proffered hand away with far more strength than he would've expected.

She moved down another couple of steps and let out little groans of pleasure as the water splashed up over her chest. Grayson closed his eyes for a moment, frozen when her throaty sounds hit him directly in the stomach, then travelled lower.

His body had always been treacherous around this

woman. Even before she had married his friend he had been forced to pretend she didn't exist to avoid the thrall she held over him.

'You've had too much to drink,' he said, trying to ignore the delicate outline of her erect nipples through the sodden black material of her vest top.

'I'd argue that I haven't had nearly enough.'

She sighed, dipping her head into the water. The movement sent Grayson's heart pumping through his chest as he dropped to his knees, then reached forward to grab her by the shoulder and pull her back up to the surface. His shirtsleeve was absolutely soaked, and her eyes were filled with mirth as she unleashed a spout of water from her mouth directly into his face.

'You're done here,' he growled, guiding her towards the edge so that he could fish her out.

The ridiculous woman was going to end up drowned if he left her in there any longer.

'You're not my keeper,' she said, eyes blazing.

The alcohol had apparently loosened the fury that she'd held back earlier, but to be honest he far preferred it over her cold indifference. She was a passionate woman, and she'd often been the loudest one in the room, always talking, moving and smiling. He shouldn't care—it wasn't his place… But it felt wrong to see her in any other way than as the tornado of passion she usually was. So if making her angry was what was necessary, he would take that hit.

'Stand up, Isabel. *Now*.'

He stood back and folded his arms, using the same cold expression and commanding tone that he had perfected over two decades in Elite One. The tone that had once got his contract terminated by a corrupt billionaire team owner, penalty-free, and that on countless other occasions had taken journalists to task when they'd dared to ask questions that invaded his privacy.

Isabel simply rolled her eyes at him.

He exhaled on a growl, easing down into a squat position as he debated just hauling her out by that pretty blonde ponytail. Sure, she'd be furious, but at least she'd still be conscious and breathing by morning.

'I can't leave you in the hot tub alone after you've been drinking. It's not safe.'

'Not safe if I'm alone?' she asked, mimicking his gruff tone. 'I think I know a way we can solve that problem.'

He spotted the spark of mischief in her eyes a second too late, and suddenly she was in front of him, her hands wrapped around his shirtfront. One quick tug was all it took for him to lose his balance and slide into the water.

He didn't quite fall so much as slide slowly. But by the time his feet hit the bottom and he'd regained his equilibrium he was submerged to the waist, with bubbling froth rising up to hit his chest.

Isabel laughed, sliding to the opposite edge of the tub to evade his potential retaliation.

'I'm fully dressed, for goodness' sake,' he growled, feeling the warm water permeate his bespoke suit trousers and handmade leather loafers.

'Would you have agreed if I'd *asked* you to strip off and hop in?' she asked sweetly.

'You know the answer to that.'

He sighed, unbuttoning his shirt and peeling it off his wet skin. He left his trousers on, to keep some semblance of decency between them, feeling her eyes following his movements intently as he unclasped his antique watch and laid it down safely, away from the edge.

'Is your…? Is the watch okay?' she asked suddenly.

'Thankfully it avoided the same fate as my shoes.'

He narrowed his eyes upon her, seeing that all trace of mirth had been replaced by a look of guilt. She knew how much the timepiece meant to him, he realised. She knew because he had told her himself one day, as they sat side by side while Luca served them imaginary tea. She'd asked, and he'd surprised himself by telling her the truth. It was the last gift he'd ever received from his father, before his death. He wore it every day, eschewing the flashier designer brands.

'I know that I'm having fun, so this must be unbearable for you,' she said dreamily, leaning her head back to twirl her hair in the water.

'You think I find fun unbearable?'

'I *know* that you find fun unbearable. Well…unless you're playing with Luca. Or with your fast cars.' She frowned, looking up at the sky through the plate glass roof that covered the length of the wraparound terrace. 'Maybe you just find *me* unbearable. I suppose my own particular brand of chaos must be less than appealing for Mr Perfection.'

'I'm far from perfect, Isabel.'

She looked at him, and her eyes seemed to heat every spot of his face and chest as she scanned him with interest.

'You just got thrown into a hot tub and your hair hasn't even moved out of place. It's inhuman. I'm convinced you're a vampire, or something.'

She tilted her head to one side, considering him for far longer than anyone else would dare. For some reason that action alone had him wanting to laugh, but he was deeply conscious of the fact that she was still in shock, and that this strange, almost humorous interlude was simply a result of her teetering on the edge of her control and trying to find some kind of solace.

And if he had to indulge in strange conversations about vampires to stop her from doing anything more chaotic than jumping fully clothed into a hot tub, then so be it.

'Actually, no…you'd be more of an animal shape shifter, I think.' She assessed him shrewdly. 'King Grayson…a powerful warrior…renowned for the speed and strength of the lion that he transforms into at will. I'd draw your eyes first…'

'You know my track nickname, I see.'

'Everyone knows who the Golden Lion is.'

Who he *was*. He felt tempted to correct her, and felt a flare of irritation at the reminder of that vague sense of loss he had felt over the past few months since his retirement. The irksome worry that without his racing persona he didn't know who he was or how to behave.

He'd walked away from Elite One because he'd achieved everything he'd set out to and the timing had felt right, but the boardroom was a vastly different environment, and he could no longer hide behind a racing helmet.

In order to show his belief and passion for what Verdant was capable of he had to show more of himself…and therein lay the problem.

He reached out to hold her upright as she leaned her head back against the edge of the tub. 'Why don't we go back inside?' he asked.

Her eyes snapped open, pinning him with their pale green depths. Like cat's eyes, he had always thought. Shrewd and all-seeing…giving nothing away of what thoughts might lie beneath.

'I don't need to be minded,' she said, her gaze showing another hint of that fury he had seen earlier. But just as quickly she closed her eyes and tilted dangerously backwards again.

Grayson was upon her in a moment, hoisting her bodily against him and deciding it was better to simply risk her anger than it was to continue with this madness.

He wasn't prepared for her to run her hands up his wet sleeves.

'I always wondered what these arms felt like without the racing suit… The night we kissed you were all covered up. They're even harder than I remember.'

Her reminder of that night caught him unawares,

sending a rush of heat deep into his gut and lower, hardening him into an embarrassingly swift erection.

He tried to shake it off, thankful that he was so practised in burying his reactions to this woman. Still, he couldn't quite stop himself from asking, 'Do you think of that night often?'

She narrowed her gaze. 'Do you?'

They remained in a silent stand-off for a full minute, neither of them willing to give in. He slowly became aware of her hard nipples, pressed tight against his chest, and froze for a long moment, shocked and unable to move. Or at least that was what he told himself as he remained still and allowed her curious hands to slide up his biceps and link around his neck.

He told himself to stop her. That she'd had an emotional upheaval. That this would make everything so much worse between them.

He closed his eyes, praying she wouldn't move and press against the evidence that he was very much affected by her, and that thoughts of the one night he'd allowed himself to taste her lips and wound up having to stop himself from making fast, passionate love to her in a darkened Falco Roux garage lingered.

'Okay, it's time to get you to bed,' he said briskly.

'To…your bed?' she asked, her eyes widening.

'To *your* bed. To sleep,' he corrected her, cursing his own stupidity at not taking that damned whisky bottle away sooner. She was absolutely sauced.

'I don't want to sleep. I'm still furious with you, you know.'

She looked up at him, her expression suddenly more serious and more lucid than it had been before.

'I know. I'm sorry,' he said sombrely.

Even if she didn't remember this conversation tomorrow, he would. And he would apologise again and again until she believed him.

She stared at him, wet curls framing her beautiful face as she chewed on her lower lip. 'I can't stop wondering…if everything had gone ahead today…if you'd been too late…what would you have done?'

A vision of Isabel, radiant and round with his child, crashed into his mind just as wildly vivid as it had been before. Only now the real woman stood before him, awaiting an answer that he couldn't give.

Because how could he admit that he'd already wondered what that child might look like without revealing that his primal reaction to the idea of such a reality had been the reason he'd had to back out of his agreement with Julian in the first place?

'I'd have honoured the agreement, of course,' he answered quietly.

'And your paternal rights?' she asked. 'Would you still have waived them?'

'If you'd asked me to, of course,' he lied.

She instantly raised one brow. 'You know, Grayson…you made a deal with Julian. You could make one with me too. We could both have what we want.'

Her words struck him squarely in the chest, spreading along his veins like wildfire. No. He couldn't have what he wanted—not when it came to Isabel and her picket fence dreams. He had long ago accepted that he was much too selfish and career-obsessed ever to be a good husband or father.

'You're young. You can remarry—'

'I'll never remarry.' She cut across him. 'I'm scarred enough after my one experience of trusting a man with my heart. Even the thought of dating makes me feel slightly ill. That's why I made the decision to come here. I want to have a child and focus all my energy on making each day the best it can be. No threat of relationship drama or heartbreak.'

'You'll change your mind,' he said, partly to her, partly to himself, to push away the dangerous lines of thinking her words were opening up inside him. Lines that were perilously close to a deeply rooted yearning he hadn't truly acknowledged until just now.

'Ugh…don't say things like that,' she said loudly, then hiccupped and swayed a little in the water. 'I'm well aware I'm tipsy, but I do know my own mind, Grayson.'

'Of course. I didn't mean that to sound dismissive. I do, however, think it's time for you to go inside before we both freeze,' he muttered, gathering her tightly against his chest.

'Put me *down*.' Her fist pummelled his shoulder for the briefest of moments—until he grabbed it and held her still. He stood up, the cold air hitting his lower half and making him inhale with shock. She obviously felt the frigid cold too, her body immediately beginning to shiver and gooseflesh spreading across the pale curves of her upper arms.

'Hell, it's freezing!' she gasped, clinging onto his

neck with renewed force as she tried to mash the entire front of her body against his for warmth.

Grayson ignored the effect of having Isabel's partially nude wet body touching almost every surface of his own and focused upon grabbing one of the robes that hung near the doorway. He managed to wrap it around her without dropping her, despite her repeated protests at being managed by him.

By the time he'd walked her step by step up the stairs her head had grown heavy on his shoulder and her speech more slurred. He knew all too well the bone-deep tiredness that often came after an adrenaline rush, and she had certainly been put through it today. Even his own heartbeat still hadn't quite returned to normal.

Focusing on practicalities, he carried her the rest of the way up to the guestroom and laid her down softly in the centre of the four-poster bed. She still wore her damp underwear under the robe, but for now it would have to do.

He would not be able to tolerate her having any less clothing on than she already wore.

She moved in her sleep, nuzzling her face into his forearm and sighing softly. He backed away, but remained in the doorway for far longer than he'd intended, wondering how things might have been if he hadn't messed everything up so royally. If he hadn't pushed her away after that kiss in Singapore…

CHAPTER FOUR

Izzy awoke to sunlight filtering in through the windows. Her head felt fuzzy and her mouth dry, but she hadn't drunk that much last night, had she? Groaning, she remembered how good an idea it had seemed to jump into the hot tub in her underwear...then pull Grayson in with her.

So maybe she had drunk a little too much.

She remembered talking and talking, the words coming out of her mouth against her will, until Grayson had pulled her out of the tub. She remembered pressing her face against his heartbeat and closing her eyes—and absolutely nothing else after that.

Groaning with embarrassment, she went straight to the bathroom and set about freshening up. She showered and donned her most comfortable leggings and oversized jumper combo, complete with hand-knitted wool socks that reached halfway up her calves, with tiny tassels on their edges.

She contemplated hiding in the bedroom until the snow melted enough for her to make her escape, even though the scent of something delicious had been wafting under her bedroom door for the past twenty minutes and her rumbling stomach had her on the verge of desperation.

She placed her ear to the bedroom door, listening for sounds of her cranky playboy host. Maybe she could just slip out to the kitchen and grab some supplies from the cupboards?

As she was wrestling with her indecision a knock sounded firmly on the door, making her let out a little yelp. Remaining firmly still, she clapped a hand over her mouth and waited, hoping that he would assume she was still asleep.

'I can hear you overthinking through this door.'

'No, you can't,' she blurted on reflex, then cursed aloud.

She thought she heard him chuckle softly as she pressed her ear to the door once more.

'We need to talk.'

She felt her insides quake at those words and the potential meaning beneath them. Her memories of what she had said last night were swishy, as if she was looking at them through a carnival mirror, but she remembered a few of the choice phrases she had uttered. Had she actually suggested that he make a deal with her? And asked him if he'd ever thought about their kiss after practically swooning over his biceps?

What on earth was wrong with her?

Yes, she had been fairly tipsy, but she had been hurting as well. She had been angry, and devastated that her hopes had been dashed, and it had brought up something impatient and furious within her that she had never experienced before. That and the way he had looked at her...

That didn't quite make sense either. Surely her drunken memory had embellished that spark of heated interest in his gaze?

Thank goodness she hadn't done anything worse than get him soaked in his own hot tub. That kind of embarrassment was something she knew she would most definitely not come back from. Because one thing was for certain: Grayson Koh was not interested in her. He never had been.

'Isabel.'

His voice held an edge, and she heard the thud of one of his hands upon the doorframe. Not an angry thump, more of a prompt.

He never had been one to wait around. When Grayson Koh wanted something, he got it immediately. Maybe it was better that she got this awkward conversation over with. With any luck the weather would turn soon, and she would be able to leave and forget all this had ever happened. Maybe once she was home she would be able to figure out what her next step should be.

'I'll be down in a moment,' she said, hoping he couldn't hear the slight tinge of sadness that had accidentally crept into her voice.

She thought of the one tiny white babygrow that she had been unable to stop herself from buying the day after she'd made her appointment at the clinic. She wasn't superstitious, but she knew some people thought that buying things for a baby early was bad luck. Perhaps this entire venture had been doomed from the start.

Yes, it would have been wonderful to have had a child. And, yes, she knew that she would have made a wonderful mother… But the idea of trawling through pages of donors and trying to select a father based on a few tiny details just felt too overwhelming. And even if she could afford it—which she couldn't—there would be the effort of actually trying to get through an appointment at another medical setting without fainting into a puddle on the floor.

As a single woman, self-employed and up until last year having spent most of her life without any fixed abode of her own, she knew that her chance of being approved for adoption was unlikely.

It was a strange feeling…having accepted a new path in her life and now having everything completely changed. But, really, was she all that surprised? Any time in her life that she had ever begun to hope for a better future things had always had a way of taking a turn for the worse. But she would figure it out—she always did. She worked best alone, after all.

The chalet's main living space looked very different in the early-morning light, with warm sunlight streaming in through the high windows. She looked down and shivered as she realised the snow had reached up past the basement level overnight. But the blizzard had passed, and you might almost be fooled into thinking you looked out at a peaceful winter painting.

Inside, the fire had been lit in the large wood-burning stove and the long dining table had been set for two at one end. Pitchers of orange juice and water lay in the centre, along with bowls of dried cereal and what she rather hopefully prayed was her favourite chocolate spread.

But upon dipping a spoon in and taking a taste, she grimaced.

'What on earth is that?' she said, half to herself.

'Sugar-free vegan cacao spread.'

Grayson appeared in the doorway of the kitchen, a white cotton tea towel slung over one shoulder as he mixed something in a bowl. To her surprise he was wearing dark jeans and a wine-coloured sweater, a more casual outfit than she had ever seen him in outside of his racing jumpsuits.

'It's all I've got, I'm afraid.' He winced. 'The last time I was here it was during race season, so I was in full training mode.'

'Ah, so you've embraced a more slovenly lifestyle in your retirement?' she said drily, trying and failing not to remember the rock-hard feel of what that 'full training mode' had created beneath his wet shirtsleeve the night before.

Get it together, Izzy.

'I didn't say that…' He walked back into the kitchen. 'I only work out twice a day now, if that's what you mean?'

Twice a day? She coughed on a mouthful of orange juice, earning what she thought was a dry chuckle from the kitchen, though she couldn't be sure.

He looked quite serious when he returned a moment

later, laying down two plates of pancakes. Gluten-free, sugar-free protein pancakes, as he quickly informed her, producing some bowls of partially defrosted chopped fruit as a topping.

'I understand the need for strict nutrition as an athlete. And, honestly, these taste great...' She took another bite for emphasis. 'But a life without any sugar? You poor man.'

As they ate they kept the conversation safe, speaking only of his new business ventures and her illustration work and how they were both lucky to be able to work remotely.

She was immensely grateful for his unspoken decision not to address the things she had said to him in the hot tub. She had been angry and hurting—always a dangerous combination for her self-control. She hadn't meant any of it, and it wasn't as if she would have accepted if he had offered to go ahead with the deal he'd made with Julian. That would have been absolutely crazy.

Grayson raised his coffee cup to his mouth, his eyes meeting hers as he sipped. She didn't know why, but she felt the moment was suspended in time, and the sudden tension in the air made her stomach tighten.

He leaned forward, strong forearms corded with muscle flat on the surface of the table. Her eyes drifted downwards for a split second before she pulled them back up, mindful of maintaining a business-like distance between them. She had worked near him for weeks before, in close contact, but of course back then she hadn't known what it felt like to have his strong hands sliding along her bare skin like they had last night.

He cleared his throat and she realised he must have spoken while her thoughts had wandered again.

Dammit, Izzy, get it together.

'Can you repeat that?' she said, her voice strained and high-pitched even to her own ears.

'I said, I have a proposition I'd like to discuss with you.'

'Okay…'

She resisted the urge to squirm in her seat, wondering if his proposition had something to do with her skiing down the mountain to the nearest hotel. She wouldn't blame him if he wanted her gone as quickly as possible. She had behaved terribly. Yes, it was understandable, considering her shock at his revelation, but she just wished she hadn't chosen to process those feelings with whisky, that was all.

'Isabel, focus.'

She sat up straight, the deep timbre of his voice sending a shiver down her spine. Her treacherous touch-starved spine.

'Last night…'

Isabel covered her face with her hands. 'Grayson, please. I hoped we could just move on from last night and chalk it up to emotion and alcohol.'

He watched her for a moment, his thumb and forefinger making a slow swirling motion on the surface of the marble tabletop.

'So when you said that you longed for a child,

without the drama or heartbreak of a relationship... that wasn't really you talking?'

'I don't know...' she lied, knowing full well that it had been her.

She had been drunk, but she had not blacked out. She remembered the feeling of her anger rising within her, of just wanting her plans to be back in place. Needing the world to make sense again, the way it had the day before when she'd had everything clear.

'You suggested I consider making a deal with you,' he said, his expression calm, yet serious, as though they were discussing stock prices.

'Of course I wouldn't really suggest such a thing.' She groaned, hiding her face behind her hands as she felt herself blush. 'That would be unfair and...wrong.'

'I happen to disagree.' He stood up, walking to the sideboard at the edge of the dining space to pick up a slim tablet. 'Your words last night made me realise a great many things. Most of all that my biggest mistake was not ensuring that you were present when my agreement with Julian was discussed. I'd like to correct that now—if you're open to it.'

Izzy felt her jaw sag a little, and her heartbeat definitely doubled its pace as he walked to her side and placed the device before her. A contract was open on the screen, and with one tap of his finger a computerised voice began to read the document aloud.

She sat frozen as she processed the phrase *pre-conception agreement*, followed by the mention of both their names and some very official-sounding jargon surrounding their future efforts to procreate.

The document covered everything, putting all major decisions under her primary control while simultaneously recognising Grayson as the child's father and affording him the relevant rights. Once the voice began to delve into heavier legal jargon she pressed the pause button, and looked up to find Grayson staring at her, awaiting a response.

'You can't honestly be serious about this?'

'I thought this ten-page contract which I had my lawyers draw up in the middle of the night might be a clue as to how serious I am.'

'Grayson, you rushed all the way here to stop me from going ahead with the insemination. You made it very clear that it was not what you wanted.'

'I came here to put an end to the deal that I made with Julian. A deal made without my ever speaking to you about it first. And as I rushed here…not knowing whether you had already gone through with it or not… I thought of the possibility of you carrying my child. Thought that if I were too late I might already be on my way to becoming a father. And my reaction to the idea of you pregnant with my baby…it wasn't a negative one. I've seen you with my godson, Isabel, and I know any child would be lucky to have you as their mother.'

Izzy stared at him, pretty sure that if her jaw dropped any further it would fall to the floor like a character in one of her favourite old cartoons.

'A baby? But you're an eternal bachelor. A playboy.'

'I am a bachelor. A devoted one, at that.' He sat

back in his chair. 'But a playboy? That makes me sound like some rich waste of space, running around throwing supermodels on and off his yachts.'

'That's not how you spend your downtime?'

'Well, for one, I don't own a yacht.' He raised a brow. 'And when it comes to women... I had one serious relationship in my very early Elite One days and quickly figured out that I'm not cut out for domestic bliss. Not surprising, considering my family life was far from traditional or happy.' Grayson shook his head. 'But last night I realised that, strangely, we both want the same thing. To have a child without the messy relationship that usually comes along with parenthood.'

Izzy nodded, her hand unconsciously rising to press against her chest, as if to try and hold in her frantic heartbeat. She was rapt. She couldn't look away from his sombre face and the emotion in his eyes. She had rarely seen him smile, so closed off was he. And yet here he was, baring this part of himself to her.

'So, Isabel...what do you say? Would you like us to create a beautiful child together?'

She fought the urge to burst into laughter. 'This is just utterly nuts on so many levels.'

'You don't think that you and I would make a beautiful child?' He raised a brow.

'You know exactly how handsome you are—that's not the thing I'm questioning here. I'm questioning the very idea of two people who can hardly stand one another coming together to create a child.' She stood up and paced the length of the table, then paused, laughing awkwardly at her own phrasing. 'Of course, I don't mean *coming together*... Obviously you mean taking the artificial route.'

'No.'

Izzy froze, whirling around to stare at him, where he still sat perfectly still and calm, one hand idly stirring more sugar into his coffee.

'No?'

'I remember you told me you have a fear of medical settings. I'm not very fond of them either, and artificial insemination seems like a lengthy and uncomfortable process. As you know, I value efficiency. With that in mind, my proposal would be for us to use the more traditional method of creating a child. One that would involve us getting into bed in the literal sense. We would start immediately. Today, ideally, going by where you are in your current cycle.'

Her brain seemed to hiccup as she picked over his words slowly, as though every phrase were sending her closer and closer to a panic attack. 'You can't possibly mean that we would *sleep* with one another?'

'There wouldn't be any sleeping involved. Not if we plan for it to work quickly.'

One dark brow quirked as he stirred his coffee again, completely at ease in himself, as though he were proposing they go skiing rather than have sex.

She opened her mouth to speak and then thought better of it. When she looked back in his direction he seemed to have stiffened, his back ramrod-straight as he brushed an imaginary speck of dust from the table.

'You mentioned that we are two people who can hardly stand one another,' he said. 'However, despite my distance, I've never claimed to dislike you. Quite the opposite, in fact. And, of course, our chemistry won't be an issue, judging by the way you kissed me that night in Singapore.'

She stiffened. '*You* kissed me first!'

Grayson stood up, taking his coffee cup across to the kitchen area. 'My point is that we clearly find each other attractive. It's a win-win.'

Izzy stopped herself from asking him to clarify that last statement, watching as he moved towards the office area that branched off the living room.

'I've emailed you a copy of the contract for you to take some time and think it over. Of course you can simply refuse, if you already know your answer.' The corner of his mouth twitched, as though he believed it incredibly unlikely that would be the case.

Izzy stood alone at the long dining table, feeling like a soda bottle that someone had shaken and shaken until she was fit to burst with so many thoughts bubbling to the surface.

Despite the effect it had had on her, she'd brushed off that kiss between them as a moment filled with adrenaline that he likely regretted.

He'd been injured in his final race of the season and forced to retire his car early, but he'd still won the overall championship. Such was the wild unpredictability of Elite One racing. She'd gone to congratulate him, finding him alone in the darkened garage as all his team mates had been up at the podium celebrating. One minute she'd been hugging him...the next they'd been kissing as if their lives depended on it. His hands had been everywhere, his mouth devouring hers. He'd been like a man possessed.

Then they'd heard some of the others, coming to look for him, and he'd simply cursed under his breath and...walked away.

She didn't know how long she'd sat alone in that dimly lit garage before she'd finally mustered the courage to walk back out and join the celebrations.

The next day, Astrid had let her go.

So he found her attractive... It was likely meant as a compliment but, coupled with how he was proposing this potential lovemaking between them as part of a pragmatic business arrangement, she had a feeling she shouldn't let it go to her head.

There wouldn't be any sleeping involved.

What exactly had her life become that she'd heard such a phrase coming from one of the world's sexiest men, right after he'd informed her that he'd like to start trying to put in a baby in her? Immediately.

Izzy covered her face with both hands and felt that she was blushing again. She walked to the patio doors, sliding one slowly open in search of some cool air, trying to calm down her raging heartbeat. She didn't know how long she stood there, staring out at the snow-capped trees, but after a while she could no longer hear Grayson's voice coming from the office area.

The thought of him walking out here to continue their discussion while she was literally burning up at the thought of agreeing to it was just not okay. Perhaps a more confident person might have stood her ground and prepared to discuss the finer details of this proposal, but while she prided herself on being a modern woman, Izzy had always been an absolute prude when it came to talking about sex.

She was awkward, and *it* was always awkward, and the very thought of having to ask him to explain step by step exactly what this was going to involve made her cringe so hard that before she knew it she'd bundled on her coat and ventured down the back stairs into the snow. She needed some time to think, to make sure she wasn't overlooking a potential misstep in all of this. She wasn't running away...not really.

Izzy felt the pressure within her chest increase until she feared that she might actually split apart, right there in the snow. The cold air was almost painful as it entered her lungs in swift gasps. Was she actually considering his offer? She didn't need to ask herself that question twice, because from the moment he had spoken, something had lit up inside her like firework. *Hope.* Hope that she had told herself not to feel.

But the way Grayson had laid it all out just felt right. Not typical or conventional by any means, but...inexplicably right. It was as though her intuition had taken one look at that ridiculously detailed preconception agreement and then rolled over onto its back and said, *Okay, let's get pregnant, Izzy.*

The realistic part of her knew that it was absolute madness to consider such an arrangement with a man who was so uptight. Let alone the fact that his proposition of them doing it 'the old-fashioned way' would involve a lot more than just learning not to fight with one another…they would actually have to have sex.

Sex with Grayson Koh was something she had definitely imagined during her short-lived crush three years ago. He'd always had a kind of enigmatic charisma without even trying to be personable. His very presence seemed to engage her—and not just because of his perfectly defined abs and smooth, chiselled jaw.

No, for her, Grayson's appeal lay in how ridiculously competent he was at everything he did. She was convinced the man could decide to build a space rocket and he would complete it on time and under budget. She couldn't help it. To her, as a walking chaos gremlin herself, witnessing his sharply focused expertise as he discussed his job was more heady than any effect his athletic physique might have.

She closed her eyes, telling herself that it was just the ovulation hormones making her instantly imagine that physique all hot and sweaty and pressed up against her. She hadn't had sex in years. She and Julian hadn't been intimate with one another after the first couple of months of their marriage, and she hadn't even tried to entertain the idea of dating since his death. Her husband's issues with addiction had often led to difficulties in the bedroom, which had affected his mood, and her confidence, and… Yeah, her sex life had been pretty much subpar up to this point.

She had a feeling that sex with Grayson would be anything but subpar.

But sleeping with him was only a temporary means to a much more permanent end. If she did this, he had made it clear that he would not be an anonymous donor—he would be their child's parent. He would be her baby's father.

She waited for an internal shift towards resistance at that idea—after all the soul-searching she had done to arrive at her decision to become a single mother by choice, surely this was a backward shift?

But he had used words like 'want' and 'chemistry'…words that had touched upon that tiny little spark of hope that lived within her chest.

The little spark that she had tried so hard to keep under control. Because it tended to blossom at the first hint of nourishment.

She would never do something so foolish as to dream of a happy ever after, like she had done in her marriage. She wouldn't even dream of any relationship with her child's father beyond platonic co-parenting. If she did this, she would be accepting an equal partner in a team of two. She wouldn't be alone in this—not all the time anyway. And she wouldn't have her child wondering who its father was and if it hadn't been wanted, the way she had wondered for most of her teenage years.

She felt as if she stood on a precipice, gazing down at uncertainty, black and swirling below.

CHAPTER FIVE

WHEN GRAYSON ENDED his call and found the living space empty, Izzy's cup of tea unfinished and abandoned on the coffee table, he got a bad feeling. Looking out at the snowy slopes to the rear of the house, he thought he could see the distinct impression of two delicate-sized footprints from poorly insulated footwear stumbling off in the direction of the hills.

Before he could think, he put on his heavy ski coat and ventured out after her. As he followed her footprints down the long, sloping garden to the rear of the chalet, he prayed she hadn't gone through the treeline and out onto the mountain beyond. His chest tightened at the thought of her losing her footing in those ridiculous boots and sliding down into danger.

But when he reached the edge of the garden and looked towards the treeline, he spied her sitting on a rock, a safe distance from any potential danger.

He stopped, exhaling hard as she turned to face him. 'Do you have a death wish?' he heard himself growl, his own fear destroying all his tact, as usual.

But he didn't care. He had seen far too many people make poor decisions when they were in shock or under pressure. She wasn't used to this terrain, and the swiftness with which one could get into difficulty here.

'I just needed to clear my head.'

She crossed her arms over her chest defensively, eyes narrowed into pinpoints, spitting green fire. In comparison with the lifeless disillusionment he had seen on her face yesterday, her anger was quite a welcome sight.

Isabel was not made for small, shy emotions. She was made to feel everything at full throttle, like an emotional engine of the highest power. Whereas he had always felt cold, reserved, and tightly wound up. He was certainly feeling wound up now. She had almost run off the side of a mountain at the first mention of him taking her to bed.

'Is my proposition so unappealing that you'd prefer the risk of falling off a snowy cliff?'

'Don't exaggerate. I just walked down to the end of the garden path.'

'In the aftermath of a blizzard,' he said, reaching forward to extend his arm for her to take. As expected, she shook her head and stood up—then immediately slipped and lost her footing on the incline.

'You wouldn't keep slipping if you were wearing appropriate footwear for the weather,' he said grumpily, grasping her hand and holding her tightly against his side.

Her eyes narrowed up at him, incredulous.

'You can glower at me, or we can try and actually

get back into the warmth before you get frostbite. Your decision.'

If she had considered shooting more fire in his direction, she restrained herself, remaining stubbornly silent as she attempted the short uphill trek back to the chalet. He felt that he was giving her footwear entirely too hard a time, considering he did actually like them. The boots suited her style, and her tough-as-nails personality. But he was angry with them for not protecting her feet appropriately, hence his snark.

He couldn't seem to control his emotions at all around this woman.

It was an unusual feeling, considering he was so completely in control of himself at all times, and had essentially made it part of his persona. In his world, where smooth reflexes and perfectly calculated turns were the difference between life and death, Izzy O'Sullivan was an unexpected obstacle on the track. Every single time.

When they reached the deck she could have let go of him and walked easily enough by herself. But he had wrapped his other hand around her waist, and neither of them made any move to pull apart—which was entirely fine with him. Without a word, he marched them both upstairs and directly into the large master bathroom.

'I can get changed myself,' she said, teeth chattering between every syllable.

He held up one of her hands to the light, hissing at the blue tinge to her skin and lips. 'Just let someone take care of you for one second, would you?'

Her mouth turned into a stubborn line, her eyes dropping towards the floor. Apparently tough love was the way to make her accept help. He would have to file that discovery away for later.

Assuming there even was a later, after he had thrust his half-baked proposition at her without warning.

He had never been a patient man; it was possibly one of his greatest flaws. The moment he decided he wanted something, he took action. And perhaps that was an admirable quality out on the tracks, or in the boardroom. But it wasn't quite so effective when it came to this fiercely independent woman.

He busied himself turning on the shower to full blast and ensuring that the temperature wasn't too hot for her. She hadn't been out in the cold for long, but the sub-zero conditions up on the mountain affected different people in different ways. While Isabel had certainly spent her fair share of time in hot climates, when she'd travelled with them for that Elite One season, he knew for a fact that she despised the cold. She was not an avid winter sportsman like he was. But, far from feeling superior, he felt nothing but anger at this damned snow for making her shiver and shake.

'I'm going to help you get undressed,' he said, keeping his voice as neutral as possible. 'Your hands are quite clearly numb, and your feet probably are as well.'

'So your solution is to help me get naked and get in the shower?'

'I'm not going to look, obviously.'

'Obviously.' She stared at a point above his head while he set to unbuttoning her coat and pulling it down her arms. She chewed on her bottom lip before speaking again. 'If we went ahead with your ridiculous proposition you would have to look at me.'

Surprise held him still for a long moment as he processed the mental image her words evoked. Shaking himself back into the moment, he allowed his gaze to rake slowly down her still clothed body.

'You think that would be a difficulty for me?'

A rosy blush appeared high on her cheeks. 'I don't know what to think when it comes to you, Grayson. I never have.'

He raked a hand through his hair, not quite sure how to verbalise his response without sending her running for the hills. How could he tell her that his offer was not just about them making a child together. That it was also about appeasing his own burning curiosity and putting to bed—quite literally—the need that he'd had since the moment he'd first laid eyes on her. The purely physical, burning lust that had shamed him when he'd realised how very innocent and idealistic she was.

The fact that he had avoided her so effectively said nothing about her and everything about him and his own lack of control around her.

But here he did not need to exercise that control…

Not if she said yes.

Not if she agreed to this wild arrangement where he would be required to perform…

And perform he would. He would not stop until he

was sure that he'd done his very best to fill her with his seed in every position imaginable—that much would be an absolute promise. But, more than that, he would make sure that the memory of how he'd got her pregnant would haunt her long after the deed had been done…

Izzy fought with her own curiosity and confusion as Grayson remained silent while he finished helping her to undress, before turning around and leaving the bathroom, as promised. She stepped into the shower, soon warming up, and closed her eyes as she tried to process the labyrinth of the conversation between them.

She had learned long ago not to waste her time trying to make people like her. Most of the time you couldn't change their minds anyway. And, sure, perhaps Grayson had never been openly hostile towards her—but he had never tried to get to know her. Not to mention the long, narrow-eyed stares he'd thrown her way whenever she was talking to others, or being chatty and sociable, as though her very existence irked him.

When she'd told Eve about it, during one of their long phone conversations, her friend had laughed and said it was probably some ridiculous form of repressed attraction. A theory that Izzy had instantly squashed, because he was a world-famous racing driver, for goodness' sake. The idea that a man like him would ever need to repress any desire he had was laughable when she had witnessed women quite literally throwing themselves in his direction almost every time he was out in public.

But even if it *had* been the case—which it most definitely hadn't—she would never have rewarded such childish behaviour. She hadn't tolerated being teased by the boys in primary school, and she most certainly wouldn't tolerate it from a fully grown man, famous heartthrob or not.

But she was going to agree to his deal. She just needed to tell him as much without completely losing her nerve.

Without another second of waiting, she got out of the shower, walked to the opposite side of the bathroom and opened the door to the master suite.

He had showered too—that was the first thing she noticed. The scent of his lime soap was heavy in the air and tiny droplets of water still clung to the edges of his jet-black hair. He had shaved, his jaw now clear of the shadow that she had noticed this morning. The entire length of the room separated them, and yet she thought that she could feel the exact moment when his eyes raked along her towel-clad form.

'Don't say anything,' she said quickly, taking another step forward, bridging the gap between them and praying that her bravado wouldn't wear off and leave her speechless and silly in such a crucial moment. 'Just…let me get this out first. And then you can do your usual thing.'

'My usual thing?' One of his dark brows rose instantly in defence.

'You're good at this…the contract talk. The way

you raised the subject, it sounded like something from a boardroom rather than a proposal for us to create a child together. To sleep with one another...'

She closed her eyes, feeling her words tangle together in the way they usually did when she urgently needed to get a point across. Typical that her mind was a swirling vortex of thoughts and words just when she needed peace, and that in the moment she actually needed it to work everything went radio silent. She pressed her lips together, opening and closing her mouth a few times, before gulping in defeat.

She heard Grayson's footsteps move a little closer towards her, but she couldn't quite force herself to look up for fear of the pity she might see in his gaze. She didn't want this to be a moment of pity—she needed them to be equals, so that she could actually accept his offer. So that she could feel empowered by doing so.

All those words had seemed right on the tip of her tongue when she had been alone in the bathroom, staring at her own reflection, but now that she was here, and he was looking at her in his usual handsome brooding way... She felt like that same little girl who had always been overlooked and rejected and made fun of. Logically, she knew that was ridiculous. Logically, she knew that she was an adult. But that was the funny thing about trauma. It didn't care for logic.

'Can I just say one thing?' he asked, and his tone was not mocking or impatient, but tinged with a softness that she was not accustomed to hearing from him.

Izzy nodded, crossing her arms over her chest

and trying not to focus on how very vulnerable she felt, standing in his bedroom in a towel while he was mostly dressed and looking a lot more poised than she did.

'I'm sorry if my wording seemed businesslike. I thought that was the best approach at the time. Truthfully, I didn't think much at all before laying it all out there.'

He ran a hand through his still-damp hair in a way that should have made him look unkempt, but didn't. The man seemed to exist in permanent male model mode—it was ridiculous.

'I'm not any more relaxed about this than you are,' he said. 'I'm just a little bit better at putting on a mask of indifference.'

She stared down at her ridiculous bumblebee toenails. 'You must wear that mask a lot, then. Because I don't think I've ever seen you look anything other than completely calm and in control.'

'I just asked my best friend's widow if she would like to be the mother of my child… I'm probably feeling the furthest from calm and in control than I ever have in my life.'

It should have been a sombre statement. It really should. But as Izzy took in this reminder of their situation, of the link between them, she had to press her lips together to stop herself from laughing aloud.

'You find that funny?' he asked, sounding confused.

'Oh, come on.' She let out another thoroughly inappropriate gasp of laughter. 'It's so utterly ridiculous. This entire thing… It's positively Shakespearean.'

He looked away, but not before she got a glimpse of what she would have bet money was a half-smile of his own. She cleared her throat, chasing away the last of the giggles, and faced him once more.

'Okay,' she said simply. 'I want to do this with you. I… I agree to your terms.'

'You do?'

'I'd already decided I was going to say yes when I was out in the garden. I just… I had to work myself up to actually saying it out loud.'

'Is that so?' He took another step forward. 'It would have been nice to be informed then. Especially as I practically dragged you back from said snow-covered garden when I thought you were running away from me.'

'I wasn't running away. I was thinking.'

'You couldn't have done your thinking indoors and away from sharp mountain drops?'

'You are so ridiculously bossy.' She shook her head, trying not to wonder if he was this bossy in bed.

'I am,' he said, jolting her from her thoughts.

It took her a long, mortified moment to realise that he was referencing her first statement and not reading her filthy mind. At least…she didn't think he was.

Izzy looked up to find him looking at her, his gaze narrowed. The air was thick with tension, and she felt awkward and thoroughly out of her depth now her initial pep had gone after her walking in here and telling him her answer.

'So... How do we go about this?'

She sat down on the end of the bed, trying to hide her shaking hands by sitting on them and crossing her ankles in a way she hoped was elegant and ladylike.

Grayson tilted his head to one side, surveying her. 'If you'd read the contract, you'd have seen that it includes my most recent health screening results.'

She nodded. She had seen that and greatly appreciated it. 'I don't have the results to hand, but the clinic had me do some tests too and I'm all clear,' she said.

'I'll take your word for it.'

Izzy inhaled a fortifying breath and forced herself to meet his gaze without dissolving into tears or more of those panicked giggles. 'You said we would start immediately if I said yes. And I think we should. Just to...to get the awkward part over with, you know?'

He didn't move, and didn't speak for a long moment, but she could hear the sound of him grinding his teeth. A muscle ticked in his jaw rhythmically as he seemed to think over her words.

'You make it sound like a chore to tick off a list. Like doing the laundry or taking out the trash.'

'I don't mean to be offensive. I'm sure you're quite good at this under usual circumstances. I just mean that this isn't a typical situation for either of us, so there's no need for us to...'

'To pretend that we're enjoying it?' he offered helpfully when she tailed off.

She exhaled a harsh breath. 'I just mean that I don't expect a big seduction or a prolonged performance. We should be practical.'

'This isn't a fertility clinic.' His eyes seemed to glitter darkly, and his lips were a harsh line—as though he were about to dish out some kind of punishment for an unknown infraction she had just made against him. 'But we can skip the seduction and pleasure…if that's really what you want?'

'Practical would be best,' she heard herself say.

If he was surprised by her answer he didn't show it. He simply stood with hands on his hips, staring down at her in his usual imperious way. To all intents and purposes, they might well have been conversing over a boardroom table rather than across his luxurious king-size four-poster bed.

Izzy gulped.

The corner of his mouth quirked slightly and he took another step closer. 'Do you expect me to lie you down right here and just get the job done?'

Izzy squared her shoulders. 'I think that would work best for me, yes. That is…if that's okay with you.'

He was quiet for a long moment, his brows knitted together in thought, before his charming smile was back in place.

'You are in control here, Isabel, so if you want the business performance… I'll will give you the business performance.'

Izzy swallowed past the lump in her throat as he took another step forward until the barest few inches separated him from where her knees rested on the edge of the bed. It was completely clear that this was to be an agreement between them, with no emotions, no feelings. So why did she suddenly feel as if she was missing something important? As though for the briefest moment he had been waiting for her to object.

After all her soul-searching over the past day, she didn't think she could take it if he changed his mind again so soon. But then again it was probably better that he changed his mind now than after they let things get any further and she became more attached to the idea of having him as her child's father.

Even just allowing herself to think of him that way… It felt so right.

This arrangement that he'd proposed was the best of both worlds, and all she had to do was get him through this part. The baby-making part of their arrangement. She could hide her attraction to him and she could school her reactions, she was sure of it. She would do whatever it took.

CHAPTER SIX

Izzy had learned long ago that if she gave herself too much time to think she got frozen up. So she knew, like taking a sticking plaster from a wound, there was no sense in prolonging an uncomfortable situation. It was easier to just pull it off.

She was about to have sex with a world-famous motor racing legend and she had tiny yellow cartoon bumblebees on her toenails.

'Something funny?' His voice was low, and seemingly calm, but his eyes didn't stray from where they were raking over her bare legs.

'I laugh when I'm nervous. Sometimes I make jokes too… Bad ones.'

'Inappropriate footwear and inappropriate jokes? I would expect nothing less from you.'

'If you mention my boots one more time, I swear I will…'

His hands moved down to his belt, unbuckling it slowly, and her words died on her lips.

'You will…?' he prompted.

'Well, I was going to say I would walk out of here right now, but that's not really going to happen, is it?'

He paused, a serious expression transforming his face. 'You can walk out of this room at any moment. Now…ten minutes from now…no matter what. You change your mind, we stop immediately—understood?'

She had been referencing the whole snowbound situation, but still she felt something release in her chest at the acknowledgement that even though she had signed their agreement she could always walk away if it became too much. She'd had to resist running from this room multiple times already, but now, as she stared at the very prominent evidence of his eagerness to fulfil the physical part of their bargain, she felt that she would stick around just a little longer.

'The same goes for you,' she breathed, hating how wispy her voice sounded to her own ears, but needing him to know that she wanted him to feel he could stop, too, if he was having second thoughts.

There was nothing typical about what they were about to do. She wasn't quite sure how he usually operated, with the long line of beautiful dates who had adorned his arm at various events, but for her sex meant something and it always had.

She had tried to separate herself from it—had tried to have one-night stands like some of her other nanny friends had. But being a nanny was a high-pressure job, with very little room to make friends or go on dates while on contract, so really it had been no surprise that she had got to the age of twenty-four without ever having had sex.

Then along had come Julian, with his charm and his declaration of true love, and she had been head-over-heels in lust. The first few times they had attempted to make love had been disastrous, with her nerves and Julian's ego taking a bruising. So it had been easy to blame herself for their non-existent sex life when he had disappeared on week-long yacht parties mere months into their marriage.

It had only been once they had separated and she had begun seeing a therapist that she'd realised how abnormal all of their marriage had been. Julian had basically wanted a fake wife to placate his parents, and he had found himself an easy target.

Grayson's husky murmur of her name pulled her from her thoughts, and she looked up to find him staring down at her with an expectant look on his face.

'I'd like to start now, please,' she said.

Her sweet little *please* ripped through Grayson's tightly wound control, the politeness of it coming from her plump pink lips almost more than he could bear.

She'd like to start now. Right here, on this bed, she would like him to begin creating their child.

He'd made his offer as businesslike as possible, and, in truth, he was more than prepared for the arrangement to proceed with no passion whatsoever, if that was the way it was destined to be. But after almost an entire year spent lusting after this woman, only to watch her elope with his best friend, he had more than his fair share of pent-up desire that he would very much like to slake.

And, judging by the darkening of her eyes when he had mentioned just how thorough he intended to be, he didn't think he would be alone in feeling that desire. Not one little bit.

Carefully, he took the final step, bracketing her knees with his own. In this position, she would have to tilt her chin all the way up to look at him. The sight of her this way… It lit up his treacherous mind with illicit images. For too long he had denied himself any fantasy of those lips, but now he leaned down, taking her chin in his hand and tilting her face up even further, so that she would have to stretch forward to meet his kiss.

He kissed a path along the side of her throat, and the taste of her skin was like hot syrup drizzling down over the sweetest plum cake. He wanted to devour her whole. But he held back, keeping the kiss level, allowing her to get used to him.

He felt her hold her breath for a split second before she gave in, the barest moan escaping her throat. The sound of it destroyed some long-held dam within him and his control slipped by the barest inch, heat sweeping along his veins like wildfire.

He had mere seconds to savour his victory before she was clawing at his chest, pushing at him frantically, as though she feared he might not stop.

With one movement he created space between them and waited.

'Why would you…? What are you doing?'

'I was kissing you,' he said roughly, resisting the urge to lean forward and continue where he'd left off. But he could tell she was determined to keep him at a distance. If he pushed again now, she'd only pull back even further.

She remained still, her eyes studiously avoiding his and her delicate hands braced against the front of his chest.

'No kissing,' she whispered.

She abruptly lay back on the bed, as though she were trying to do it quickly, so as not to lose her nerve. And with every prim tug that she gave to her robe to cover herself his confidence lessened. His fantasy of unwrapping her slowly and savouring the delicious revelation of her nude skin before tasting every creamy inch no longer seemed within reach.

Suddenly he felt less sure about his decision to partake in this arrangement. This morning everything had seemed so simple. He would have his cake and eat it too. He would have the child he longed for, while also getting a taste of this maddening woman he knew he could never let himself have for real. But now, faced with her determination to hold him at arm's length, he wondered if perhaps he was only digging the knife in further by having her this way without truly having her at all.

Whenever he'd allowed himself to imagine taking her she had felt what he felt, and she had been longing for it just as much as he had. But this real version of Isabel was distant and determined to keep their arrangement under control, and he had to respect that—even if he knew that she had wanted this too, once. He had seen it in the way she'd looked at him whenever they'd been alone together. He had felt it on the night that they had almost given in to that desire before fate had stepped in and ruined everything in the grandest way possible.

His intuition had never steered him wrong in his entire life. Not on the track, not with his business endeavours, and not even with his one disastrously failed relationship. When his gut told him something, he listened and he took control. And he won—every time. But Isabel needed to be in control here, and he needed to tell himself that he was just going along for the ride. He would take whatever she gave him and it would be enough. It had to be.

He spread her thighs wide, praying that she would be wet enough to take his girth. He usually took pleasure in the prelude to sliding inside a woman, but she had made it more than clear that she didn't want him to do that.

As he placed himself against her entrance, the feeling of her hot bare flesh was so intense it sent a shiver of pleasure up his spine, almost undoing him before he'd even begun.

He groaned, and when he spoke his voice was strangled as he fought to hold himself still. 'I need a moment... I can't—'

She stiffened, turning her face away from him. 'It's okay. You tried.'

'I tried?' Grayson frowned down at her, taking in

her awkward posture and her refusal to meet his eyes. 'You think that *I'm* the one having difficulty here?'

She stubbornly kept her head turned away from him, her chest still rising and falling fast and her cheeks flushed rosy pink. 'Aren't you?'

'Isabel… If you think that I'm not fighting off every instinct that's within me to take you right now, to open you wide and accept everything you're offering me…'

'I don't understand…'

He realised that she didn't. Isabel had absolutely no idea that he'd been about a second away from an embarrassing release, simply after that first touch of his erection sliding against her soft skin.

So soft… So painfully perfect and surpassing every one of his dreams…

Suddenly his insistence on completing their deal 'the old-fashioned way' felt less like an indulgence and more like an exercise in torture. The most painfully perfect torture he had ever endured. But he didn't want to endure it. And he didn't want her just to endure it either. He wanted her to enjoy it.

'My research told me something very interesting about increasing the chances of conception…' he said, increasing the pressure of his pelvis against hers. 'Would you like to hear it?'

'Yes…'

That single word came out almost like a moan, hardening him even further, but he remained still, resisting the urge to thrust against her like a rutting animal.

'We're far more likely to be successful if it's not just me who…reaches the finish line.'

'Did you just use a racing pun in lieu of the word orgasm?'

'Is orgasm the word you'd prefer?' he asked, with as much patience as he could muster with her staring up at him, green eyes wide and uncertain.

'I… I don't know.'

For a woman who always seemed so self-assured in her day-to-day life, this lack of confidence in the bedroom set off alarm bells in his mind. He fought against the anger he felt in his chest at whatever had happened to make her feel this way. She was trying to deny her own needs, minimising herself to a mere spectator, and he wouldn't have it. Not with him.

'There's no rule to say we can't be practical and still enjoy this, Isabel. And I think you'd enjoy me making you come…very much.' He inhaled a breath of her delicious scent. 'I could take it nice and slow with my mouth…or I could get you there fast with my touch. Whatever you want. Let me get us both there.'

She inhaled a swift breath, her pretty pink lips pursing as she turned away. When her gaze finally returned to his, her pupils were wide and her lids heavy. His words had created that reaction. Could it be that she'd enjoyed a little dirty talk…? Interesting. Very interesting…

On the track, a millisecond's delay in reaction had the potential for disaster. He was a master at observing that and reacting under pressure. But he didn't think he'd ever felt more pressure than at this moment. It should be simple, he told himself. It was just business, after all. Right?

Perhaps it was selfishness, or bravado, or his own ego, but he needed Isabel to enjoy this. He needed to know that his attraction hadn't been one-sided all those years ago. If he had any chance of laying his own fixation to rest, he needed this to be right.

He met her gaze head-on as he trailed his fingers down her stomach, emboldened when she didn't look away this time. 'You said you don't want me to kiss you and I won't…' he said, his voice a husky whisper. 'But I can't promise that you won't beg me to.'

'I don't beg,' she said roughly, gasping as his fingers finally reached their destination.

'I'll remember that,' he murmured. 'I don't need to kiss you to get you there. I'm quite thorough. And when I set myself a goal… I like to win.'

CHAPTER SEVEN

Izzy could feel her heart beating in every point of her body. Grayson was barely touching her, and yet it felt as if he was everywhere. His mouth almost touched the sensitive skin beneath her ear and she fought not to groan aloud. His teeth grazed its sensitive shell for a split second and she felt her entire body shudder against him, her hips moving upwards of their own accord.

He let out a thoroughly masculine growl of approval, his own hips pressing back against hers. The delicious hardness of him was right there, pressing against her upper thigh, and she thought that she might convulse into flames upon the spot.

'This is better,' he murmured against her ear. 'Do you like your breasts to be played with?'

'Um…yes, please.'

'So polite, Isabel.'

His breath fanned against her neck, his eyes meeting hers for a split-second before he trailed his hand down the centre of her chest and parted her robe.

She was in a haze, in some kind of dreamlike state

where nothing made sense, and the most handsome man on the planet was undoing the tie of her robe as though she had just given him the keys to a bank vault.

She looked at him and realised he had frozen at the sight of her naked breasts, bouncing free from their silk cover. He liked her breasts—that much was certain. He wasn't a good enough actor to pull off that kind of reaction. The realisation that he hadn't been lying when he'd said he was attracted to her was both unsettling and intensely erotic.

He didn't wait for another breath before encasing one entire nipple with his mouth. No gentle teasing or nuzzling. As though he knew it was exactly what she wanted. He sucked and laved the sensitive tip, kneading one breast with his hand while his wicked mouth teased a slow, sensual torture upon the other.

A loud moan echoed in the darkened room, and it took her a few moments to realise that the sound had come from her own throat. She froze, embarrassed, immediately wishing that she hadn't agreed to his ridiculous mention of an orgasm. It would take too long, it wasn't necessary, and she needed this to be done with.

Unable to speak such words aloud, she settled for guiding him with her hands as best she could, until he got the message and positioned himself firmly between her thighs. Like this, there was no denying the power of his muscular frame against her own much softer curves. They were so different, worlds apart, and yet when he finally pressed his length against her none of that seemed to matter.

His expression was stark when she looked up at him, his jaw tight as he entered her in one slow thrust. He moved slowly, filling her and then retreating, with smooth, shallow thrusts that sent stars bursting behind her eyelids.

Izzy inhaled a soft gasp at the instant build-up of pleasure in her core with every flex of her inner muscles around his hot length. He paused, angling himself upwards before his next thrust, and Izzy fought the urge to cry out as he rubbed against that perfect spot deep inside her. Her hips moved of their own volition, needing more and more of whatever magic he was working between her thighs. But as another raw moan escaped her lips she froze again.

Keeping her distance seemed utterly laughable in the face of the pleasure he was wringing from her body after just a few short minutes. It was far too much...and yet nowhere near enough. Was this how sex was supposed to feel? This intense, insatiable hunger?

'You still with me?'

A hand reached up to touch her cheek, jolting her from her spiralling thoughts. Grayson's dark eyes pinned her in place, his strong hand coming to brace just below her jawline. For a moment she thought he might try to kiss her again, and she both wished he would and wouldn't all at once. She felt as if the world had turned upside down and she was no longer in control.

'Tell me what you need,' he said, his body poised like a statue above her.

His hard length was still buried deep inside her, but he didn't move an inch as he awaited her response. She couldn't hide herself away—not from Grayson. He easily held himself in check, his patience and strength evident in the stillness of his rippling muscles.

You might think that driving a car around a racing track would lead to you being able to look whatever way you wanted, but that wasn't the case. Elite One drivers were among the fittest competitors in the world. And she had this driver all to herself in this snowed-in cabin. It would be anyone's dream. And yet here she was, trying to talk herself out of the physical reaction that she was having with him.

Maybe he was right. Maybe they should use their mutual attraction to their advantage. It didn't have to be clinical. Maybe she should take this as a chance to explore the things she'd always been afraid to ask for before.

'I need you to…go a little…harder, maybe,' she said, gasping when he seemed to grow harder inside her.

'Like this?'

He withdrew slowly, tightening his grip on her hips before sliding back home with one sharp thrust. Izzy gasped and saw stars.

'Or like this?'

He spread her thighs wider, angling one arm on

the headboard above her before repeating the motion with even more effort.

With a gasping, 'Yes!' Izzy scored her fingers down his smooth chest, earning a loud growl of appreciation.

There was no more talking after that. She was lost to the sensation of being possessed by him as he found that spot within her once more and refused to let up until she was crying out in the most powerful climax of her entire life. She vaguely heard his words of praise as he continued to move inside her, seemingly determined to hold off on his own release.

'This is what you need?' he demanded, his thrusts slowing as he sought her gaze. 'This is what you want from me? Show me, beautiful… Take it from me.'

It took her a moment to realise what he meant, and then she was moving, angling herself up against him and meeting him thrust for thrust. She was stunned as another climax began to build inside her, but she was determined to hold off. The pleasure of moving against him was so intense. He growled as he found his release, spilling himself into her with a shocking heat that sent her hurtling straight into another orgasm.

Breathless and exhausted, she was only vaguely aware of Grayson propping a pillow under her hips, murmuring something about her not moving for a while.

That would not be a problem, she thought, catching her breath, considering her entire body was boneless. And then the sleeplessness of recent days caught up with her and she drifted off peacefully to the sound of Grayson's wry chuckle.

Grayson's morning workout had taken twice as long as usual for him to complete, so consumed was he by the effect last night had had on him. His punishing twice-daily strength training sessions had been the only thing keeping his sanity intact since he'd found himself stepping away from competitive motorsport after two decades. But today, with every mile he ran on the treadmill in his high-tech home gym, he had to fight not to go in search of Isabel and ask her for a repeat performance.

Accepting the end of his Elite One career had been a complex process. Much harder than he had anticipated, as he had learned to cope with less travelling from country to country across multiple time zones and climates, and no more hectic testing and racing schedules, not to mention never-ending sponsorship commitments and press appointments. It felt like going through withdrawal. But his drug had been the rush that came from constantly being on the go.

Now he'd retired, he suddenly had as many days off as he wanted. It had been welcome for a few weeks, but after that boredom had set in. And because of his natural competitive spirit, it hadn't take long for him to begin looking for fresh challenges.

He hadn't known what to expect from Isabel this morning, after she'd come apart for him last night, but this little game of cat and mouse was not it. Although, really, was he surprised?

She had all but admitted to being celibate these past few years, and he'd responded by taking her fast and hard as if they were teenagers having a quickie.

He closed his eyes, remembering the feeling of sliding into her for the first time…watching her try not to react to him. Her efforts had been in vain, as he'd known from the start. She'd softened under his touch like butter, and he'd devoured her like a starving man offered his first meal. Feeling her perfect body respond to his touch, hearing her little sounds as he'd filled her all the way that first time… It had been too much, and it had been over far sooner than he'd been ready to accept.

Then afterwards he'd felt completely undone. He'd wanted nothing more than to slide into bed alongside her and doze, until they were both ready for round two, but she'd made it quite clear his job was done for the day. It had been a rude thump back to reality and he had responded in his usual bullish fashion. He would be avoiding himself too, if he were her.

The problem was, if she wanted to get pregnant she would have to come and find him eventually, before her three days of optimal fertility were up. Their chances would only increase with the frequency of their lovemaking, after all.

He paused the treadmill. Yes, that was something he definitely needed to remind her of…immediately.

After taking the world's fastest shower, he pulled on a pair of loose grey sweatpants, opting to wait a moment before putting on his T-shirt. It might be shameless, but if her open adoration of his body was the only arsenal he had in this battle of wills he was going to use it. He hadn't earned his reputation of being ruthless without reason, after all.

He prowled along the lower floor, seeing no sign of blonde curls or long legs.

There were too many levels in this house—too many rooms for her to hide in.

But the sweetest aroma wafted on the air, coming from the main living space, making his mouth water instantly. The kitchen was tucked behind the formal dining room, and as he neared he could hear soft humming.

She had her back to him, and a large mixing bowl balanced in the crook of her arm as she stirred with a wooden spoon, round and round. She didn't hear him come in—she was far too busy singing along to something playing in her earbuds, her hips swaying softly from side to side as she worked.

Isabel was not a natural singer. He had found that out one sunny summer afternoon when Luca had asked them both to sing nursery rhymes with him. She had joked that what she lacked in actual ability, she more than made up for in pizazz. Her off-key crooning had sent his godson into fits of laughter, and he'd only barely managed to hold his own stern expression in place. Of course his lack of reaction had only encouraged her to sing louder, her pink cheeks matching the bright streaks of colour that had accentuated her riot of blonde curls at the time.

He frowned at the memory, remembering how

carefree she had been. How she'd made him wish he could be the same.

Somewhere over the past few years she'd lost that fire. He wanted it back.

He waited for her to turn, to catch sight of him in her peripheral vision, and sure enough her entire body stiffened. Gone was the dancing and the swaying, and back came that damned distance.

'Sorry, I should have asked before I went digging around in your kitchen.'

'Don't apologise. Not when it makes my house smell like this.' He stepped further into the kitchen, seeing that she had laid out three full trays of circle-shaped biscuits. 'Were my healthy protein pancakes not to your liking?'

She smiled, ducking her head as she looked at the first batch of cookies on the cooling racks. 'You may be used to a boring athlete's regime. I, however, still require a daily dose of sugar for my sanity.'

'Boring?' He gasped, placing a hand playfully over his heart.

'Perhaps disciplined is a better word. Discipline is necessary, of course. But I firmly believe that nothing tastes better than what you think is forbidden. Especially when it comes hand-frosted.'

She lifted up one of her finished confections and, sure enough, he saw the plain circle had been transformed into a tiny snowflake. As he watched, some of the icing dribbled onto her fingers and she licked it off. He exhaled on a slow hiss, feeling himself instantly become hard.

'Want a taste?' she asked innocently.

She had no idea.

He moved at lightning speed, grasping her wrist and sliding his tongue slowly from the centre of her palm up towards the tip of her fingers. The taste exploded on his tongue and he groaned, fighting the urge to bite into her flesh. Not a hard bite…just a little one. He had a feeling she'd like it too.

A barely audible moan escaped Isabel's lips as he tested his theory, scraping his teeth gently against her skin as he worked a second path back down.

'I meant the cookies…' she breathed, still not making any attempt to remove her hand from his grasp.

'I know.'

With a herculean effort, once he'd finished cleaning the sticky icing from her fingers, he removed his lips…and waited.

'I'm pretty sure you just seduced my hand,' she whispered. 'How is that even a thing?'

'You offered me a taste and I took it.' He held her gaze. 'Besides, I agreed to forgo seduction, remember?'

'That felt pretty close to seduction.' She licked her lips. 'You're not playing by the rules.'

He popped the remainder of one deliciously frosted cookie into his mouth with another groan, and felt deep satisfaction when her pupils widened at the sound.

'You said nothing tastes better than what we think is forbidden? I say that when we make the rules, we get to decide when a situation requires breaking them.'

'What rule would you break first?' she asked curiously.

'You know which one.' He took a step closer, narrowing the distance between them until her amply curved bottom was pressed up against the kitchen cabinets. 'Tell me to seduce you. Tell me that while you're here in my bed for the next three days you're mine. Let us both take all the pleasure we want from each other. The pleasure you deserve, Isabel, if you want it.'

Her eyes closed at his words. 'I want it...'

'Then open your eyes and touch me,' he demanded, needing to know that she was there with him in this. Needing to know that when he took her this time, she would be giving in to the craving just as much as he was.

She trailed her hands down his bare chest, taking her time as she caressed his skin inch by inch. When she began to explore his erection through the thin material of his sweatpants he cursed under his breath and stilled her exploration, lifting her up until she was perched on the kitchen workbench.

'Can I kiss you this time, Isabel?' he asked, framing her face with his hands.

She hesitated, chewing on her lower lip. 'I think I'd like to keep that rule, if we can?'

He nodded once. Disappointed, but not entirely surprised, considering how he'd behaved the first time he'd kissed her all those years ago. How quickly he'd lost control and then abandoned her.

How could he tell her that he had carried his regret about that night for the past three years? That it was like an ache in his bones, accompanying him through every day? He'd behaved badly…shown her exactly why he was the wrong man for her…and all the while he'd foolishly hoped she'd see through the act. That she'd *see* him and feel some level of what he felt.

No, it hadn't been a simple attraction. There had never been anything simple about what he felt for Isabel.

He skimmed his fingertips over every inch of her, avoiding the perfect lips he craved. He nipped at her skin with his teeth, removing each item of her clothing in a slow torture, and making good on his promise to show her *exactly* what it meant to be seduced.

By the time he finally slid a finger into her slick folds she was plump and begging for release. He obeyed, taking another firm bite from her shoulder as she screamed her climax and collapsed backwards against the marble countertop. Grayson spread her wide, sliding into her molten heat as he stared into her pleasure-drunk eyes and wondered if *enough* was a concept that would ever apply to this woman.

He needed to show her that in his bed…in his arms…she was *his*.

He needed to make her crave him.

His own orgasm built swiftly, his hips pistoning hard and fast as he worked to give her every last drop of his release. Closing his eyes as he came, he resisted the urge to claim her lips as he wanted to. To break down all her walls and demand more. But that wasn't fair. He wouldn't fool himself into thinking that they could have anything more than this, but he could ensure she was satisfied.

Taking her by the hand, he guided her to his bedroom, where he thoroughly intended to keep her until their deal was completed. Two more nights was what he had, and two nights was all he would take. But he would make the most of every damned second.

CHAPTER EIGHT

FOR TWO WEEKS Izzy threw herself into work. The fantasy novel illustration package was the kind of thing she had grown used to being able to complete with minimal issues. But every day she grew more and more distracted and restless.

It was strange that for all the months when she and Julian had, as she now knew, been fruitlessly trying to conceive a child, she had been hyperaware of her body's signs, counting down each day on her calendar with a borderline obsessive frequency. But that since her plane had landed in a snowy Dublin and she had driven herself home to her tiny cottage to sit alone in the silence, she had only been thinking of one thing.

Grayson.

The few days she had spent in his chalet, in his bed, in his arms…

It had changed something within her.

Once she had realised that her marriage to Julian was a sham, she had been relieved at the idea of never opening herself up to anyone. Why on earth would she? Why would she risk her heart being broken by someone she loved?

Not that she would ever be so foolish as to fall in love with Grayson, of course, but she at least trusted him enough to create a child with him. She'd trusted him with her body, with her pleasure. People talked about *risking* one's heart, or *falling* in love, as though romance was some kind of extreme sport. For Izzy, trusting someone felt much more dangerous than loving them. Unrequited love could break your heart, but trusting the wrong person could ruin your entire life.

The enormity of how her life might be about to change had been weighing heavily upon her mind—so much so that she had almost completely blocked out the idea of their efforts actually working. But now the day had arrived and her period was due. She hadn't been able to muster the energy to walk into her local chemist and procure a pregnancy test, knowing that in such a small town it would lead to people asking questions that she wasn't quite ready to answer.

Eve and Moira had welcomed a healthy baby daughter shortly after Isabel's return, so she'd opted not to fill her friend in on the updated details of her own baby-making efforts. But yesterday a care package of sorts had arrived, containing chocolates and a full packet of pregnancy tests ready to go.

Grayson had been in contact a handful of times since they'd parted ways in Zurich, when he had scolded her for not accepting the use of his private jet. Such a wasteful luxury, she had told him, scandalised that he owned one but not entirely surprised.

She had told him that she would be testing today and that had been it, really.

It shouldn't hurt that their communication was based solely around her potential pregnancy, but her brain and her heart couldn't seem to reach an agreement on that.

So the day had arrived, and with it the moment of truth. She slid open the simple packaging and read the instructions. Nothing about this was glamorous… nothing at all…

She performed each action with an almost detached efficiency until there was nothing left but the four-minute wait that would seal her fate.

She was pacing the bathroom when the sound of the doorbell rang out across the cottage. Looking at her watch, she frowned, knowing that the post was never delivered on a Sunday and she had no unexpected guests here, ever, such was her position on the outskirts of town.

A tall, dark shadow was barely visible through the smoked glass of her front door, and she felt her heart begin to beat a little faster. One peek through the peephole had her scrambling to open the door before she'd even had a chance to breathe.

Grayson stood in her tiny portico, his collar turned up against the light Irish rain that had created a dull mist along the rolling hills behind him.

'You're here…at my house…' Her words were a stunned whisper even as she fought the urge to smile. Because Grayson was here, on her doorstep, looking as gorgeous as ever. And, fool that she was, she had missed the sight of him.

'I thought perhaps you might like company…in case there's cause for celebration.'

Izzy felt her chest deflate a little at this reminder that he was not here for her, he was here to check in on his investment. It felt rather cruel to refer to their potential child in such businesslike terms, but the alternative was to romanticise their situation—and that was not an option. Nothing had changed. Even though for her it had felt as if it had for a moment back in his bed.

She ushered him inside her narrow hallway, scrambling to push her hastily discarded muddy Wellington boots out of sight. As if on cue, the scrambling of paws sounded and Sasha came running at full speed to greet their guest.

'No, Sasha, down!' she chided, easing the over-eager dog away from Grayson's perfectly pressed slate-grey trousers. 'Sorry, it's my elderly neighbour's dog. I her walk sometimes. She still hasn't quite mastered the art of the polite greeting.'

Grayson chuckled and got down into a crouch to scratch Sasha behind her ears. Izzy could do nothing but stare. He looked so impossibly handsome at that moment it threw her for a loop, and her brain stuttered to a stop.

For a man so feared for his ruthlessness, it seemed he was gorgeously soft with small creatures of all species. He'd hidden this softness away so tightly, always concealing it beneath that formidable racing driver persona. She wondered what else he hid of himself, and if she would ever truly know the father of her future child. Because she knew without a doubt that with every tiny piece of himself that he revealed, the more she wanted to see. And that was a real problem for their platonic parenting arrangement.

She sagged back against the wall a little, praying that he would say something predictably cold, just to set the world back to rights again. But, alas, Grayson stood up and took a look around her tiny cottage and smiled. Not just a tiny ghost of a smile, either. The man had *dimples*.

She was pretty sure she felt the final barrier around her heart drop, shattering on the ground around her at that revelation.

'It looks exactly how you described,' he said, walking further into her cramped living room and touching a few of the tiny statuettes that she'd placed above the fireplace. 'You said you did all the work yourself?'

She had said that, hadn't she? During their last night together in the chalet they'd stayed up talking until dawn. She'd found herself telling him about her childhood, and about what a big deal it had been, buying her first home after essentially being homeless for most of her life.

'It's no fancy ice palace or Monte Carlo villa, but it's home.'

'I see now why you found my decor lacking,' he murmured, sliding his hand along the bookshelves, where she kept a mixture of her favourite fantasy novels and some of her most prized artwork. His hand stilled over one of her childhood drawings she'd managed to keep, his fingers tracing over the messy crayon lines.

She'd told him about her childhood habit of drawing a huge house on a hill, with four square windows at the front and one big red door. Every time she'd been moved to a new place she'd drawn that house and imagined herself living in it with a family of her own. She'd learned that her imagination could be a place of solace. That she could create her own world by opening a book or taking out her crayons. Art had been her sanctuary, and she still tried to hold that knowledge close every time she embarked upon a new project.

'I didn't say it was lacking, did I?' She hid a smile behind her hand, turning to walk into the kitchen.

He followed closely behind. 'You didn't. But I bet you were thinking it…weren't you?'

'I wouldn't dream of insulting your delicate ego that way, Mr Koh.' She laughed good-naturedly, letting out a long exhalation of breath before turning back to face him in her tiny kitchen. 'But mostly I'm panicking over what on earth I can offer you to drink. I don't have fancy coffee or artisan pastries.'

'You don't need to offer me anything, Isabel.'

'I'm Irish—these are the rules. So I'm going to make tea—proper tea, unlike the tripe you served up in Zurich—and then we can look at the…' She froze, planting one hand quickly upon her forehead. 'The test!'

She heard him follow along behind her as she raced into her tiny bathroom and grabbed the white stick from the vanity unit.

'I've already done it… I was waiting for the results when you arrived.'

'Do you want me to leave?'

Izzy shook her head. 'This is as much a big deal for you as it is for me.'

She took a deep breath, unwrapping the test from the cocoon of toilet paper she'd left it in. Nerves swooped around her stomach like butterflies. This was it. This was the moment when she would find out if they had created a child together. And if they had then there would be no need for them to continue seeing one another outside of routine doctor's appointments until the baby was actually born.

That was the plan, she reminded herself.

She placed the white stick on the counter in full view of them both, then exhaled the breath she'd been holding as she processed the two little words in plain text on the screen.

Not Pregnant

Grayson stood by her side, but she didn't dare look up at him. Not when a riot of emotion had unleashed itself within her chest, making her hands shake.

She suddenly wished she'd been alone, as she'd always been before when doing these tests. She'd only ever had to deal with Julian's disappointment via text or passive aggression, even though she now knew that had all been fake and manipulative, as she'd never have got pregnant by him.

But before the voices within could begin telling her what a mistake this entire venture had been, Grayson met her gaze in the mirror. She couldn't quite make out the emotion blazing in his eyes, but he certainly didn't look disappointed with her, or angry.

'Well, that's that, then.' Izzy forced a smile, turning to face him. 'It didn't work.'

'It didn't work *this time*,' he said, that shrewd gaze seeing far too much. 'I'll have to try a little harder on my next visit.'

She felt heat rush through her at his words and the image they evoked. It made no sense; she should be upset that she wasn't pregnant. She waited for the familiar wave of inadequacy to come, but instead she was horrified to realise what she was actually feeling was…*relief*. Relief that for one more month at least she would be the only woman in Grayson Koh's bed. And that made her more confused than ever.

She knew in that moment, with all her heart, that she was most definitely in trouble.

If Grayson had already been unsure of why he'd travelled all the way to Ireland, when Isabel had said she'd be quite content to send him the test results via text, then he was even more unsure as to why he'd insisted on taking her out to lunch.

The wet and winding Irish country roads proved to be a surprising challenge to navigate in the clunky rental car that he'd managed to nab at the last minute. But Isabel was comfortable in the passenger seat, laughing as she instructed him to drive far away from her small town to avoid any local busybodies asking questions about her famous guest.

If any of the other Elite One drivers could see him now—oh, how they would laugh. He imagined driving these roads in one of his own cars, with the wind whipping Isabel's curls around her face. The image his mind conjured was so clear and so *right* that it shocked him for a moment, and his jaw clenched almost painfully.

Thoughts of her had consumed him with increasing frequency as he'd awaited news of their baby-making results. Of course a selfish part of him was happy that he would have another chance to bed her for three nights, as per their agreement. He'd already begun to plan where those three nights might take place. But the more he tried to place his attraction to her in that perfectly labelled box, the more his mind seemed intent upon wanting something else.

He looked across to see Isabel staring serenely out at the passing green fields and wondered how today might have gone if the test had been positive. If the 'business' part of their arrangement had already been completed and they'd moved on to the part where he'd see her only for doctor's appointments and then as per their arranged co-parenting schedule.

His jaw tightened as he pulled up where Isabel indicated.

'The food here is good, but not very fancy...'

Isabel bit her lower lip, looking suddenly unsure

as they stepped out of the car and gazed up at the thatched roof of the mountainside pub.

'I said that I wanted to experience authentic Irish cuisine.'

'Okay, just try not to draw too much attention to that handsome face of yours. I'm starving, and I don't fancy having to wait hours for you to sign autographs.'

'Why do I suddenly see why Luca always instantly fell into line around you?'

'Strict boundaries with a heavy dose of empathy. It works.'

'Lead the way.'

He tried hard to ignore the sudden tightening in his jeans as she swirled and sashayed those glorious curves ahead of him into the warm pub.

The interior was just as quaint and fundamentally Irish as the exterior, with polished stone floors and a high fireplace dominating one end of the large open dining space. Posters and memorabilia covered almost every spare inch of wall space, showing advertisements from times long past and famous Irish musicians and poets. It was a renowned tourist spot, apparently, as evidenced by the busy air of the place and the myriad languages he could hear being spoken among the tables as they walked through.

He had only ever visited Ireland twice before, on fleeting press trips, and he had loved the people's lack of interest in celebrities then just as much as he did now.

The flow of music and chatter around them formed

a charming cocoon as Isabel guided him through the traditional Sunday lunch menu. They started with a creamy vegetable soup, served with freshly baked Guinness bread and possibly the most delicious butter he had ever tasted in his life. It was golden in colour and slightly salted, and he was pretty sure he moaned a little as it hit his tastebuds.

Izzy tried to hide her smirk behind her napkin, but he saw it and answered it with his most stern expression, which only made her smile even wider.

Next came tender thin slices of roast beef, dressed in a rich gravy and served with creamy mashed potatoes and steamed garden vegetables. The presentation was no-fuss, the flavours simple, and yet he enjoyed it more than the food at some of the most highly rated Michelin star restaurants he'd eaten in. It helped that there were no judgemental gazes upon him as he ate, no unwritten society rules that he might inadvertently overstep. These were normal people, enjoying a relaxing meal with loved ones before the working week began anew.

He thought it was much the same as the way his own life had been before his driving career had skyrocketed, but he could hardly remember it now.

'Now, tell me again that Irish cuisine isn't a thing?'

Isabel was sitting back, patting her stomach with satisfaction. She smiled at him, her eyes sparkling in the pub's dim lighting, and he felt something tighten in his stomach in response.

'I stand corrected.'

His smile was forced now, but if she noticed his

sudden tension she didn't comment. He was glad, because he couldn't explain it himself.

They both declined dessert, having planned to follow the signs for a scenic walk along the mountainside—only for the skies to open out of nowhere, soaking them both to the skin by the time they ran back to the car.

The Irish weather was just as temperamental as the feisty blonde beside him. He had already seen blistering sun and hail today, and he had barely been in the country more than a few hours.

The drive back to Isabel's cottage passed with her telling him about her latest book cover commission, for a young adult fantasy novel filled with monsters and magic. She lit up when she spoke about her work, and the new techniques she'd had to master in order to get it just right. He got the impression that she was a perfectionist with her craft and that no one pushed her harder than she did herself—something he could definitely relate to.

When they arrived at her home, he found himself walking her to her door despite her protests. She paused on the doorstep, fiddling for a moment with her keys. It reminded him of the kind of awkward first date aftermaths he'd seen in teen comedy films.

'I'm glad you were here today.' She spoke softly, staring out at where the sun was beginning to lower on the horizon. 'I know your schedule is crazy. There was no need for you to come all this way for nothing.'

'It wasn't for nothing. And I don't do anything that I don't want to do, Isabel.'

He hesitated, not quite wanting to reveal exactly

how much he had been haunted by thoughts of her over the past couple of weeks. How his mind had been invaded and his body overheated at the mere hint of the memory of their few nights together. He knew he wanted more time with her than just the bare minimum, but that was the one thing they'd both agreed not to do.

He had entered into this arrangement with the perfect balance of control and distance. Isabel would be the ideal mother for his child, with no risk of divorce or drama. Every moment he spent with her like this was a risk that she would begin to view their relationship as something more, and that would be disastrous for both of them.

He checked his watch, knowing that he needed to get to the airport soon or risk having to reschedule his flight to Singapore.

He had thought he was taking control of his desire, slaking his lust for her while still benefiting from their orderly deal. He'd wanted to make her crave him. But in reality it was probably the other way around.

'I hope that your new love affair with Irish butter made up for it just a little,' she said. 'I don't think I've ever seen someone eat it directly from the packet before.'

'I'm debating having a crate ordered, so I can take it with me whenever I'm travelling.'

She laughed, but something in it sounded a little hollow. 'You still do quite a bit, even now you're retired, right?'

He nodded.

She bit down on her lower lip, considering her words for a moment. 'Grayson, I need you to know that if you've reconsidered our arrangement at all—'

'I haven't.'

'I know you haven't *now*, but conceiving can take a while for some people, and—'

'Have I done something to make you doubt our agreement, Isabel?' he asked, taking a step closer to her in the cramped porch.

Up this close, he could see the tiny flecks of gold in her hazel eyes, and the dash of freckles on her nose and cheeks. She stared up at him, her pupils widening in the way he remembered. He wondered if she was just as turned on as he was right now…just as aching for release.

'Of course not. You were… You've been amazing.' She inhaled sharply, rosy dots appearing on her cheeks. 'I mean, you've been very thoughtful and patient, and I'm happy to try again, as we agreed.'

She blushed again, and he felt a flash of heat in his abdomen. Was she already anticipating it? Was she also secretly thrilled that they weren't 'one and done', as he'd promised her so confidently?

He'd never been so relieved not to win at something—not that it was a race. The way they'd made love back in that snowbound chalet had felt more like an exercise in endurance. He'd felt aches in his body for days afterwards, every twinge reminding him of how he'd wrung every ounce of pleasure from her eager body. How she'd opened to him completely and trusted him to show her true pleasure.

He reached out, the barest touch of his fingers on her jaw, to guide her eyes back to him. 'You were amazing, too.'

Isabel leaned in, surprising him with the softest kiss on his lips. The first she'd given him since that one night three years ago.

It was like being bathed in sunshine, and the heat spread along his skin instantly, warming him to his bones. He hadn't even realised he was cold. But just as quickly as she'd leaned in, she stopped and pulled away.

'Sorry, I just…'

He pulled her right back to where she belonged, swallowing whatever apology she'd been prepared to offer with a kiss of his own. But while her kiss had been soft and sweet, his was filled with raw hunger and demand.

She'd told him no kissing, and he'd obeyed. But now that she'd broken her own rule all bets were off. He held her right where he wanted her, her soft waist bracketed between his hands, as he plundered and took with sensual ferocity. Punishing her, punishing them both with everything they had agreed they couldn't have together. This wasn't about their deal—this was about them.

When he finally raised his head and looked down at her he was satisfied that she looked just as affected as he felt. They stared at one another, breathless in the fading evening light. She exhaled a long breath, but didn't look away. Her pupils were blown wide with desire, her lips swollen from his.

He reached out, running a fingertip along the damp flesh of her lower lip, and she shivered. 'Tell me to walk away again…and I will,' he said.

'I know.'

Her admission was all the permission he needed to gather her up into his arms. He'd never seen kissing as more than a prelude to lovemaking. But he could have kissed Isabel O'Sullivan for hours, right there on her doorstep, in full view of the street. Let the neighbours gossip. He didn't care about anything right now other than getting this woman to the nearest bed.

He needed her complete attention. He didn't think he could bear any more of her smiling deflections— not when he felt as if every inch of his carefully crafted armour had been ripped apart. She had got under his skin with her steadfast refusal to be impressed by the trappings of fame and wealth. She was everything that he had studiously avoided for decades, while he'd kept his focus where it needed to be, but now he'd had a taste of her and he had no idea what anything meant any more.

All he knew was that he wanted more.

CHAPTER NINE

ISABEL WAS ONLY vaguely aware of how she and Grayson got through her front door and along her cramped hallway while kissing one another as if they were on their last breath.

One of his hands was in her hair, holding her in place, while the other soothed along the side of her neck. His mouth was hot and frantic on hers, his lips and tongue working a delicious rhythm upon her control.

She was the first one to pause, gasping for air, while Grayson simply growled a protest and continued his path of sensuous torture down her neck.

'Isn't this breaking one of our rules?' she forced herself to ask.

'Not my rule.' His voice was a husky murmur against her skin. 'And you broke it first.'

She had, hadn't she? She knew there was a reason why it had seemed important to kiss him, but as Grayson seemed intent on driving her wild with his sinful mouth she couldn't seem to muster any resistance at all. In fact, she urged him on, with her fingers in his hair and her body writhing under his expert touch.

This was what she'd denied herself back in the chalet. This intense sense of connection was what she'd
known she needed to hold at bay. But she could no
more tell him to stop now than she could deny herself
air. His hands moved to grip her by the belt loops,
pulling her flush against the very hard evidence of
his arousal.

'Sorry.'

He froze, angling himself away from where Izzy
had been more than ready to have him. Pressed hard
between her thighs.

'Don't be…' she breathed. 'I liked it.'

Her words seemingly placated him, but still he
didn't grind against her like she wished he would. He
retained a maddening distance away, keeping their
contact to slow, drugging kisses. When she took him
by the hand to lead him towards her bedroom, he
stopped and lay her down on the sofa instead. Where
they kissed some more, still fully clothed.

It was simultaneously too much, this deep kissing, and not nearly enough. Surely what they had
done in Switzerland should have felt ten times more
intimate? Ten times further across the invisible line
drawn between them in the sand? But this moment…
whatever this was…felt like something new. What
had happened between them before had been a part
of their arrangement. Using their mutual attraction
to their advantage, as Grayson had said.

But this… She had no idea what they were doing
here. No idea why he had chosen to spend basically
an entire day in her very non-glamorous area of Ire-

land, eating pub food and running through the rain. Her head swam with confusion and wonder, and her long-buried inner romantic scrambled to find meaning in his actions.

'Grayson… You don't have to be careful with me, if that's what you're worried about. I'm here. I want this.'

He stared down at her for a long moment, his expression thoroughly unreadable in the lamplight. His hand cupped her jaw, his fingertips sliding slowly along her sensitive skin. 'I didn't come here for this.'

'We don't have to do anything.'

'No, believe me, there is nothing I want more right now. Nothing I have fantasised about more for the past two weeks… I just mean I'm not expecting you to do anything you're not comfortable with. Just because we've done this before.'

That tiny romantic within her came roaring to the surface, punching her fists to the sky with hopeful optimism. He had thought about her. For the past two weeks he had been haunted by their time together just as she had. He wasn't unaffected. She had no idea what any of that meant for them, for their arrangement, for anything… But right now Grayson was kissing her because he wanted to.

There was no chance of them creating a child tonight. If she was to make love with him right now it would be just that—two people finding pleasure in one another's bodies, bringing each other to the dizzying heights of climax simply because they desired it. Because they desired each other.

She pulled him back down to her, taking his mouth in a kiss that was far more assertive and dominating than any of her others. She felt bold, ablaze with heat, and hungry for this man. She wanted him so damned much.

And, yes, while she might have had him many times in their snowbound chalet, she had never before had the knowledge that even if they hadn't had their agreement he would still be there. That she would be the woman he chose to have in his bed right now. And although they might not currently be in a bed, she had him here on the sofa, looking at her like that… She didn't plan to waste a single moment.

'I need to know what you're thinking,' he growled.

'I'm thinking that we're both wearing far too many clothes.'

'Is that so?'

She made a murmur of agreement and he rocked against her, his hardness against her soft core sending bolts of electricity along all her nerve-endings.

Her T-shirt was pulled over her head less than gracefully, and she barely had a moment to catch her breath before Grayson's mouth was on her breasts.

'There you are,' he growled, his lips latching on to one hard peak.

'Did you just address me…or my breasts?'

'They made quite an impression on me last time.' He looked up at her, his smirk lopsided.

He took his time wringing pleasure from her, with slow strokes of his tongue on her skin and his fingers working magic between her legs. He had learned what she liked very quickly, and he had retained all that information, systematically bringing her to a bone-shattering orgasm in less than two minutes. He looked up at her, and the smile on his face was one of complete satisfaction.

The rest of their clothes weren't so much removed after that as ripped from their bodies with a complete lack of patience. She was pretty sure she heard buttons ping onto the wooden floor as she impatiently pulled his shirt front apart.

His dark chuckle turned quickly into a growl of approval as he finally sank down on top of her naked form. She was breathless, and wanting, and yet she still had a moment of stunning clarity, gazing up into his beautiful face and seeing his expression soften as he finally entered her. With each slow thrust she felt herself begin to come apart all over again, but she didn't want to be alone this time. She wanted him right there with her.

'Come one more time for me, Isabel,' he urged. 'I need to feel you.'

So she did. She came on a silent scream, glorying as he roared his own release and came to rest in a heap on top of her.

Neither of them moved for a long time, their ragged breaths mingling into one until the chilly night air began to make her shiver. She was vaguely aware of Grayson carrying her into her bedroom, perhaps with the intention of going to sleep, only for her hands to begin wandering the moment they both lay under the covers.

'You're insatiable.'

He chuckled, but didn't stop her in her explorations. He simply lay back, watching as she set about showing him just how insatiable she was. She teased and worshipped him with her mouth until he lost patience and pulled her on top of him, where she rode them both slowly to the peak all over again.

Grayson slid out of bed just before dawn to the sound of his phone ringing from somewhere on the other side of the cottage. He hissed under his breath as he bumped into numerous surfaces in the dark, finally finding the device in the pool of clothing he'd discarded earlier.

He winced at the bright light of the display, sobering when he processed the name of the caller.

'It's early, Astrid,' he rasped. 'I hope this is important.'

His close friend and PR manager's cool tones filtered down the line. 'It would be afternoon if you were in Singapore as scheduled, Grayson.'

'I made a last-minute change to my travel plans.' He kept his tone light, not offering up any details, but trying not to lie either. 'It was a personal matter. I haven't missed any important events.'

There was a long pause on the line—a sign he knew only too well meant that either bad news was incoming or he had royally messed up and she was calling to tell him off. He guessed at the latter.

'Is this "personal matter" the reason why social media has been abuzz with rumours that you're currently zipping around the Irish countryside with a mystery woman? My phone hasn't stopped ringing.'

Grayson stilled. 'Are there photographs?'

'Just some very grainy ones of you in a pub. I'll send the link.'

The photo came through instantly—a side profile of himself smiling. Other than a flash of blonde curls, Isabel was mostly obscured by the wingback chair she'd been seated in. He hadn't seen anyone taking pictures, but of course there would have been someone who recognised him. He wasn't that naïve, was he?

He leaned forward on his knees, looking around at the cosy living room that Isabel had worked so hard to transform. He knew all too well how quickly his presence could bring the hounds right back to her door. And yet he had still chosen to come here, selfishly wanting to see her again.

'Well? What am I telling them?' Astrid asked.

He rubbed an agitated hand across his face, his voice coming out as much more of a growl than he'd intended when he answered. 'Tell them nothing. No comment. I'm on vacation.'

'You know that won't make it go away...' A pen clicked in a slow, steady rhythm in the background. 'First you race out of those meetings in Monaco and refuse to tell anyone where you're disappearing to. Now you're off on an impromptu sojourn around Ireland...'

Grayson scowled at the knowing tone in his friend's voice. Astrid hadn't made her way up from being a personal assistant to become the most in-demand PR manager in motorsport for no reason. She still worked for Falco Roux, but she'd agreed to continue to represent him after he'd retired. She knew damned well that he was hiding something. It was her job to keep a handle on some of the biggest egos in motorsport; she had honed her skills and could smell a lie a mile off.

'Sometimes I value my privacy in these things, Astrid,' he said, ignoring the pang of guilt in his gut at such an obvious deflection. But at least it wasn't a lie.

'Okay…' He heard the confusion in her voice, laced with just a little hurt. 'Well, I suppose I can deflect the questions for now. But you know that not turning up to these public appearances will only lead to more speculation. And we can't afford that right now.'

'I know.' He pinched the bridge of his nose. 'I'll be there.'

'Just let me know if you're bringing anyone along to these events,' Astrid said, her tone calm now, bordering on cajoling. 'Privacy is fine when you can get it, but you know that some good press wouldn't hurt right now, Grayson. You'll have to share details of your mystery lady eventually.'

Grayson felt his gut tighten as he disconnected the call, realising that in all his negotiations with Isabel they hadn't really discussed how they would navigate the public nature of his life. She had said she wished to remain separate from his world, yes. But what if that choice was taken from them?

Astrid was right. He couldn't bank on keeping his connection with Isabel private for ever. Not once they'd had a child together and he was flying back here frequently. But he wasn't about to jeopardise her trust by putting anything about them in the spotlight just yet. Whether she wanted to step back from the scrutiny of the public was for her to decide.

'Is everything okay?'

Izzy's sleep-husky voice came from the doorway behind him and Grayson jumped as though burned. The room was dark, but he saw the way she stood a little more stiffly than usual, as though she wasn't quite sure what she'd walked in on.

'Just a call from Astrid,' he said, noticing that she still didn't relax. If anything, she tensed even further.

He inhaled a breath of her cotton-fresh scent, taking in her sleep-mussed hair and the oversized superhero T-shirt she must have thrown on before coming to find him. She looked cute as a button—and yet all his filthy mind could drag up were images of how fast he could have her naked and screaming out his name beneath him on this sofa. He hadn't heard that particular sound anywhere near enough times to satisfy him yet...

'Is something wrong?'

Isabel interrupted his X-rated thoughts, her eyes not quite meeting his as she fiddled with the hem of her T-shirt.

'She was calling because I was supposed to be on a plane to Singapore last night for a charity race.'

She looked up, staring down at him. 'Grayson… you should have gone.'

'Do you regret asking me to stay?'

'No. Of course not,' she said quickly. 'I just mean… We said we wouldn't let this arrangement impact on anything else. Your career comes first.'

Her practical words should have soothed the restlessness within him—so why did he find himself pulling her closer, until his thighs bracketed her knees?

'That wasn't the only reason Astrid called. Some photos of us having lunch at the pub yesterday have appeared on social media. Don't worry, you aren't visible,' Grayson said slowly. 'But she wanted to know if she could spin my mystery woman…for good press.'

Isabel stilled. He felt her body tense under his hands, her weight shifting as though she intended to move away. For a moment he contemplated pinning her in place, but in the end he let her go. Sure enough, she was on the other side of the room in an instant.

'I said no, of course,' he added, cursing himself for how terribly he was handling this.

'Okay.' She nodded, her arms wrapped around herself.

'Is it?' he asked, standing up and clearing the distance between them with rapid strides until he was close enough to touch her again. 'Because you look very much not okay right now.'

'I didn't think this part through,' she said, her voice weak and wispy. 'The fact that you're *you*. How idealistic it was of me to think I could keep my life private if you're a part of it.'

Grayson closed his eyes, hating himself for this oversight almost as much as he hated whoever had posted that picture of them online. But she was right. It was completely unrealistic to think they could avoid this ever happening again.

'I'll understand if you want to reconsider our deal,' he said.

'No,' she said quickly, a few curls shaking loose from her messy hair. 'I don't want to do that... I just think that maybe we both need to think a little more practically.'

'I can protect you to a certain degree, but I cannot guarantee your privacy any more than I can guarantee my own.'

'But we can control how we appear to the media,' she said thoughtfully. 'How we spin it, I mean.'

'That's my reality. That's not something you or our child should have to deal with.'

'That's the reality I'm signing on for, whether we've planned for it or not. Surely it's better to get ahead of any scandalous story with our own version? For the press, for our friends? We're going to be co-parents for a long time... I'd prefer to tell our child that its parents had a short-lived fling rather than have to disclose the strange truth of this arrangement, wouldn't you?'

'A fling?' he said slowly.

'A *fake* fling,' she clarified, taking a deep breath. 'I could come to Singapore with you and we can pretend to be together while I'm there.'

A whole week of having Isabel in his arms and in his bed? Where did he sign up?

He prepared himself to heartily agree to her new proposal, but then he noticed the anxious look on her face. Instantly he got the feeling that whatever she said next would be decidedly less fun than the sex-filled montage that had taken over his imagination.

'Grayson…last night we came a little too close to breaking all the rules of our agreement.' She set her shoulders, taking another deep breath before delivering her final edict. 'If I come to Singapore with you, there can be no more sleeping together outside of our arrangement.'

CHAPTER TEN

THE MOMENT IZZY had uttered her agreement, Grayson began making calls. Izzy's suggestion that she book her own flight and follow along in a few days was met with a look of abject incredulity.

Ignoring the pit of growing panic in her stomach, she showered and dressed, then pulled out her small purple travel case—just like she had done countless times back in her nannying days. She had developed the perfect last-minute travel wardrobe over years of being on call to busy jet-setting families. A few day dresses, suitable for the humid Singaporean climate, some walking shoes, and the one evening dress she owned, black and reliable.

She held it up in the morning light, catching sight of the distinctly frayed hem, and frowned. She'd poured all her funds into renovating her home, and she hadn't really needed to update her wardrobe. Especially not so that it was suitable for being thrust suddenly into the spotlight on the arm of a world-famous racing driver. It wasn't ideal, but it would have to do.

She turned to find Grayson standing in the hall-way, watching her pack, with his phone still pressed to his ear.

'She'll need dresses for events too,' he said to who-ever was on the other end of the line, his eyes scorch-ing her skin with the ferocity of his slow, lingering perusal. 'Set up some private appointments.'

'Grayson…' She reached for the phone, embar-rassment heating her cheeks.

He placed his hand over the phone briefly. 'Isabel. Let me spoil you.'

She escaped into her bathroom to finish dressing, trying to ignore the calming murmur of Grayson's husky voice as he finalised the rest of their travel plans and a busy event schedule.

He continued to field a series of calls on the short drive to the airport, and she was reminded that things moved quickly in the international motor racing world.

The private jet was luxury such as she had never encountered. From the moment they had arrived at the small airfield just outside Dublin, she'd felt as if she'd stepped through a looking glass into another world. She'd considered herself accustomed to the ways of the kind of wealthy families she'd worked for. She'd occasionally even travelled business class with Astrid and Luca, as it had been easier for the little boy to sleep on long-haul travel, but now, as she was guided along the length of seating areas and bedrooms on this jet, she had to consciously stop her mouth from dropping open.

The jet was more like a penthouse hotel suite than a form of air travel. It came complete with a five-person crew, a gourmet meal service, full-sized beds and luxurious leather seats that most definitely would not require her pinching her sizeable hips against her neighbour's armrests. Each seat was placed at a comfortable distance from the next, with its own television screen and everything else one might need to keep track of business in the sky.

She felt Grayson's eyes follow her as she moved down to the private bedroom cabin, sitting down on the queen-sized bed to test its firmness with a little bounce.

'It's exactly like a normal bed,' she said, resisting the urge to sprawl out on what felt like million thread count sheets.

'Were you expecting rocks?'

'I thought planes had weight limits and stuff. I've only ever seen one of these on TV.'

'I find it hard to believe you never travelled like this with Julian.'

She ducked her head, the reminder of Grayson's assumptions like a chilly breeze upon her excitement.

'I paid for all the flights we took myself, before I moved back to Ireland. I only found out he was cheating on me because he used my credit card for a first-class flight to a yacht party in Miami. He hated flying commercial, but he had no money, so…'

She shrugged, realising that she had said far more than she'd meant to. Speaking of his best friend like that…it felt like a risk to the fragile truce they'd en-

tered into. But she was done with lying about the
past, when it had taken so much energy for her to
move past it.

Grayson's expression was stark. The silence between them was heavy with tension as he visibly
struggled to speak. 'He was lucky to have you. Even
if he didn't appreciate it at the time.'

'If he was raised in this kind of luxury, I can see
why it would be hard for him to fly any other way.
Still, I've got to point out that sleeping in a bed in the
sky without being strapped in just seems utterly reckless. I assume they *are* actually used for sleeping?'

'It's like being in any other bed, Isabel. It can be
as safe or as reckless as you wish.'

She processed his words in her mind slowly, bringing up a vivid image of Grayson's long, toned body
covering hers while the clouds swept past the windows and the white noise of the jet's engines muffled
the sound of her moans...

Izzy bit down hard on her inner cheek to stifle
a very real groan to match the fictional ones in her
mind. Grayson was still watching her far too closely,
and she prayed he wouldn't see her blush as she tried
to shoo away that image.

But just as quickly as he'd followed her, he retreated to the cockpit, to speak with the two pilots,
giving her space to set up her things in a seat across
the aisle from him and buckle in for take-off.

If she had felt any worry about being tempted to
join the mile-high club it was swiftly quashed when
Grayson announced that they would be making a stop

in London to pick up a few of the other drivers who were competing in the charity race.

The first, a British former champion in his fifties, now a well-known sports commentator, came on board with his wife and their two very shy and awkward teenaged sons. The reason for their shyness became apparent when the second driver who embarked directly behind them turned out to be a stunning brunette in her early twenties.

Isabel already knew who Nina Roux was—like most of the world did. Her family's Monaco based racing team and its financial woes had been all over the news lately. The historic Monegasque car brand, which had been bought out by a playboy billionaire and rebranded as Falco Roux, had nabbed Grayson as their main driver for his final few seasons, and had been none too happy when he'd made his shocking retirement announcement.

After some polite small talk, the three drivers predictably segued into a discourse on racing, leaving Izzy to strike up a conversation with the teens and their mother. It turned out one of the boys was an avid fantasy reader, and Izzy was all too happy to show off some of her work until the time came for everyone to buckle in for take-off again.

To her surprise, at the very last moment, Grayson slid down into the seat beside her.

'I got carried away talking shop and almost forgot about my nervous flier.' His gaze was soft as he enveloped her hand in his and brought it to his lips for a gentle kiss.

'You didn't have to…' Her words died away as she looked up to find they were being watched closely by their companions.

Right, we're playing the part of a couple here.

Her stomach clenched at the reminder that this week would have plenty more of this.

Grayson remained perfectly attentive and charming throughout the remainder of the flight, only just drawing the line at following her into the bathroom. A fact that was noticed by the other two drivers, who looked on with rather bemused smiles.

'I never thought I'd see the day the Golden Lion would become housebroken,' the older man remarked loudly, when Grayson could be seen pouring her tea and fetching a blanket for her cold feet. 'Hats off to Miss O'Sullivan.'

'They make me sound like a pussycat.' Grayson raised an amused brow in her direction, his hand coming to rest on her thigh in another mark of firm possession. 'Tell me, my love, have I lost my edge so soon?'

'You're still quite ferocious, darling, I'm sure.'

The endearment had slipped past her lips, setting her pulse skittering into a gallop. Grayson's answering smile made her heart beat even faster—so much so that she had to stand up with the excuse of needing the bathroom.

It took another ten minutes for her to calm herself enough to return to the cabin, where she discovered the lights had been lowered for sleep and Grayson had set up their seats to recline side by side.

It was going to be a long flight.

* * *

By the time the pilot announced their descent into Changi International Airport, Izzy had managed two long naps in between some work on a mock-up of her next illustration project to send off to her client over the coming week. Her monthly cycle was always at its worst on the second day, and she was certainly feeling its effects.

The others disembarked ahead of them, eager to make their way to their various hotels and recharge. The warm air was heavy and fragrant in her lungs as she made her way from the jet to the sleek chauffeur-driven car that awaited them on the Tarmac. Grayson had said that one of his press officers would join them, to brief him on his schedule for the next few days. But neither he nor Izzy had been prepared for Astrid Lewis to step out of the car.

'I decided to come and greet you both myself and save us an awkward public reunion.'

Grayson visibly flinched, looking briefly back to where Izzy stood, frozen at the bottom of the jet's stairs.

'Let me handle this,' he said in a low tone, his hand briefly touching her cheek in what she knew he meant to be a comforting gesture.

The touch, intimate as it was, only served to deepen the smug smile spreading across Astrid's lips.

'You didn't actually think you could keep this a secret from me?' Astrid said, her heels clicking as she strutted slowly towards them, pointing one red-tipped finger in Grayson's direction. 'I knew something was up the moment you went tearing out of that meeting in Monte Carlo. There's only one other time I've seen you lose your cool like that.'

Izzy caught a small glimpse of Grayson's almost panicked expression before Astrid shook her head with a laugh and redirected her attention to her.

'Izzy…you have no idea how glad I am to see you here.' Astrid spoke directly to her. 'I've wanted to call you to apologise so many times. I should never have let you go. I understand that you probably hate me…but I'd like to try to make amends.'

'I don't hate you. You just did what you thought best at the time.'

'And I apologise again. This time in advance. I may not be able to contain my excitement.'

Her excitement?

Izzy fought to retain a neutral expression as her former boss bypassed Grayson and enveloped her in the kind of hug that she'd only ever had from Eve in the past.

The embrace lingered, and when Astrid finally pulled back she thought she saw the tiniest glimmer of moisture in the other woman's eyes.

'Be warned: Luca will not be able to contain himself.'

'Luca is here too?' Izzy said, her voice a breathless whisper, feeling one step away from a full-blown panic attack.

This was too much, too soon, and she was completely underprepared. Grayson, on the other hand, had plastered a serene smile on his face as he accepted a hug of his own from his PR manager.

Izzy had wondered at the closeness between the two of them when she had begun working for Astrid, but had quickly realised that their friendship was like a family bond. Astrid had described to her Grayson's care towards her and Luca when she had been cast out from her own family as a young single parent. Really, that should have been Izzy's first clue that Grayson Koh was not the man he seemed to be from his public persona.

'He wouldn't dream of missing Uncle Gaga's big Legends race. He's back at the hotel,' Astrid said, her eyes never leaving Izzy's. 'If you want to see him, of course. I don't want to assume...'

Izzy held back the lump in her throat as she thought of the little boy she had cared for for almost an entire year. He would be nearly six now. She had always prided herself on keeping a professional distance from her young charges. Being almost a part of someone's family, in the role of nanny, it could be easy for the lines to get blurred. From the beginning of her time with Astrid and Luca it had been so easy to see herself as more than just a member of staff. But in the end she had been the one to get hurt, and reminded of the reality of her place in their lives.

'I would love to see him,' Izzy said now, hearing the small break in her voice. 'I've missed him so much.'

Astrid pressed her lips together, her own training in the public eye far too iron-clad for her to do something so silly as to cry. But still, the slight tremble in her lower lip as she looked away was all the confirmation that Izzy needed to know that she wasn't the only one feeling the emotion of the moment. That she'd been missed, as she'd missed them both.

'Right, now that's all cleared up….' Astrid smiled at them both, a gleaming pristine smirk that meant business. 'Let's discuss our plan to launch this fairytale to the press!'

Grayson should have predicted that Astrid's plan would be in part a punishment for his recent evasion over his private life. She accompanied them to his modern mansion in the affluent Sentosa Cove district and quite literally set a timer, giving them precisely thirty minutes to freshen up and return to the car for their first scheduled event.

He'd had plans to talk to Isabel about their living arrangements while they were here, and to discuss her preposterous wish for them to refrain from sex until the next window in their contract agreement. But when he entered his guest bedroom and looked at her face, unguarded and thoroughly exhausted, he realised that he wanted nothing more than to send her to bed—to sleep.

While it was bright and early here in Singapore, it was the middle of the night in Dublin, and he couldn't be sure how well she had slept on the flight.

She instantly refused his suggestion, of course, and their first stop was a private press conference, where Grayson was booked to formally announce his intention to launch his own team in the next year's season of Elite E. It was a move that not many could have predicted, considering he'd never discussed his interest in the engineering side of the sport, nor his part ownership of Verdant Race Tech.

When the conversation moved on to his personal life, with some questions about how his retirement was going and the recent photographs of him and his mystery woman he found himself freezing up.

Isabel sat in the back corner of the room, beside Astrid, out of the line of fire from the journalists awaiting every titbit of new information.

He was supposed to be saying what he had agreed with Astrid, but suddenly his old persona returned with full force, clamping down and freezing out every personal question that was thrown his way with ruthless efficiency. He saw Astrid's brow furrow, and the small shake of her head warning him that this was going badly. He knew he needed to return to their plan, but he was strangely powerless to stop himself.

By the time the press conference ended, and he was ushered out through a side door into the green room, a thin sheen of sweat had erupted upon his brow. His heart hammered in his chest, and he reached for the closest glass of ice water, gulping it down in an effort to regulate the riot of feelings within him.

'What on earth was that?'

Astrid burst into the room, her face a mask of thinly veiled shock and irritation. Isabel followed closely behind, her expression one more of pity than anything else. He didn't know which bothered him more.

Like always after these conferences, he simply wished to be left alone. He hated this part of his career and always had—the intrusions and demands upon him, the media waiting for the tiniest glimpse of weakness so they could exploit it.

'Could we have a moment alone?'

The request came from Isabel, and to his surprise Astrid simply dipped her head and retreated from the room. But not before delivering a tight-lipped warning that they had ten minutes before the car left for the next interview, of course.

Grayson paced the room, his hands in his pockets. For a moment Isabel simply watched him, grabbing her own glass of water and sipping delicately. Then she cleared her throat, capturing his attention, and motioned for him to take a seat alongside her.

'Is this some kind of misguided attempt at chivalry?' she asked. 'Or is there something else going on here that I need to know about?'

'You've seen what it's like out there. You know about the pieces that were published about you when you were with Julian. I can't do that to you again.'

'I think that's my decision, don't you?'

'Of course I know that it's your decision.'

'The entire reason I came here is to create the illusion of a normal relationship between us, Grayson. So that when…if…a pregnancy is announced, there's no big scandal. The press always want what they can't have. They already know something is being kept from them, so surely controlling the narrative with our own version of the truth is better than them following us around looking for gossip?'

He shook his head, hearing what she was saying but not able to accept it. Not when she didn't know the full story.

'The first year I raced in Elite One, the press got hold of my father's debt history. They decimated him in the press, painting him as a con man. And it was my fault. My press officer at the time advised me to play upon my parents' working-class roots to my advantage. So I gave an interview, waxing lyrical about how my father had scrimped and saved to pay for all my karting expenses when I was a kid. I had no idea that he had taken money from Peter Liang to pay off a bad debt.'

He shook his head, hating himself all over again for his naivety.

'After Peter Liang had stepped in and cleared my father's debts he told me that I raced for *him* now. He was starting his own Elite One team in Singapore— the first one that had ever been created there. He wanted to win a championship and he knew Julian wouldn't be the one to do it for him. He wanted me. I didn't realise for a very long time that it had likely all been orchestrated from the beginning. I had raced with Julian as a kid. I knew his father well. I knew that he could be ruthless. His father liked me, but when the time came and he asked me to sign on to their team I said no. I wanted to enter an Elite One team on my own merit.'

'That's why you never talk about your involvement in the technical side of things? Your business interests? Because you don't want the press to use it against you?'

'Exactly. I've learned that if I give them nothing, they get nothing.'

'Yes, but hiding yourself like that all the time… Trusting no one and working yourself to the bone… That can't have been easy.'

'Spoken like someone who has direct experience?'

She dipped her head, a small smile spreading across her lips. 'You always see far too much of me, don't you?'

'I don't understand how others can look away.'

She inhaled sharply, attempting a weak laugh, but he saw the shiver of unease in her eyes. He didn't want his truth to make her uneasy…he didn't want to push too hard… But when she spoke to him like this he felt his ability to refrain weaken more and more.

'We'd better get going or Astrid will probably have me retrieved by the police.'

'I hope I've helped you a little,' she said quietly. 'I don't want this trip to be in vain. I already feel like my appearance here is cramping your style somehow. I know you're probably used to a more high-flying, fun-loving type of trip when you're in your home city, so please don't change anything on my account.'

He stood up, reaching down a hand to pull her from the sofa.

'You are not an inconvenience, Isabel O'Sullivan. You are my fake girlfriend. And you will be treated to a grand tour of the city in a style that befits your position.'

She laughed aloud at his formal tone, and the sound carried him through the rest of the afternoon's meetings, where he took her advice and tried his best to lower his mask just a little.

It turned out it wasn't as hard as he'd thought to be honest—to a certain point. He would never give unfettered access to the press. He was not a fool. But he didn't have to pretend that he was something he was not either.

He saw Isabel smiling as he gave detailed answers about the new technology that Verdant was engineering for the next season. And when they asked about his mystery lady he gestured to her, seated at the back, where she was fully prepared and accompanied by Astrid.

But when Astrid announced that his appearance was obligatory at a foam party that night, at a well-known rooftop nightclub, he drew the line.

Isabel's eyes were red-rimmed, which gave him a direct insight into how hard she was working to conceal her exhaustion. His working schedule over the past two decades, and his experience of switching seamlessly between time zones while remaining fully alert and able to perform, had given him stamina. But Isabel didn't have that to fall back on. So when Astrid suggested that Isabel get dolled up and attend the event with him, Grayson put his foot down.

He escorted her personally back to his home and ignored the flicker of unease in his gut as she bade him a weary goodnight.

CHAPTER ELEVEN

Izzy AWOKE TO the dawn light filtering in through the floor-to-ceiling windows. Or at least she assumed that it was the dawn light. But in fact when she took a quick glance at her phone it turned out to be almost midday.

Jumping from her bed, she rushed out into the hallway and listened for sounds of Grayson, only to find the house completely silent. He had told her he didn't employ a large staff when he was in town, preferring to have maximum privacy.

When she looked at her phone properly, it was to find a text from him.

Got in late and had to leave early for the track. The kitchen is fully stocked. G x

She analysed the tiny x on her phone screen for much too long, wondering if it had been a mistake. Wondering if he automatically signed off that way with everyone in a text. His email sign-off hadn't ever included any tiny kiss symbols…but then again maybe it wasn't meant to signify a kiss at all. Because why would it?

She looked down at her bare feet and realised she'd been unconsciously pacing the length of the open-plan living room area while staring at her phone like an angst-ridden teen. With a deep breath, she sent back her reply, apologising for sleeping late, thanking him and wishing him luck—with no kiss. Then she stared at both messages some more, knowing that she needed to put her phone away and go in search of food.

She could go for a swim. Or maybe spend the day reading. There was no rule to say they had to spend every waking hour together.

Still, she couldn't help one more quick look at his social media accounts, just to see what he had got up to the night before.

It appeared he had attended the foam party, as planned, and then Grayson had stayed alone for the musical act that had followed—a 'famous' DJ Izzy had never heard of.

She clicked through a series of photos tagged with Grayson's name, telling herself that it wasn't snooping because technically it was public knowledge. Image after image showed him flanked by beautiful women in bikinis who seemed to be removing his shirt as the crowd around them became more and more submerged in thick white foam.

She zoomed in on the images—then froze at the wave of unbridled possession coursing through her body. With one decisive click she closed the app and placed her device face-down on the counter.

This was his life, she reminded herself. He was doing nothing wrong by attending a party and dancing. He had promised her that they would remain exclusive for the purpose of their arrangement, and she trusted him in that promise. But still… Old feelings resurfaced, from a time when she had been weaker and more fragile. A time when she had trusted someone at his word and been proved wrong in the worst way.

Grayson's Singaporean villa was part modern home, part work of art. A beautiful infinity pool bracketed the house, surrounded by tall trees that offered maximum shade and privacy. She remembered being here for a barbecue when Astrid had attended the Singapore Elite One *premio* during the year she had been Luca's nanny. She had been just as amazed by the house then as she was now. It was an architectural masterpiece of wood and glass that you couldn't help but be awestruck by. The pool and outdoor areas had been landscaped with care, providing the perfect entertaining space for its wealthy host and his many parties filled with many beautiful guests.

A thought struck her, and she pushed it away just as quickly. It was none of her business how many other women Grayson had brought here. Just as it would be none of her business once their time together had come to an end. The sooner she realised that, the better. She was beginning to feel possessive over him in a way that could only spell disaster for them both.

Refusing to wallow, she took action, responding to a series of client emails and updating Eve on her trip so far. It was still night-time in Ireland, so she didn't call her friend, knowing that she was likely still riding the high of her new baby with her beautiful wife. She was happy for Eve, she truly was. Her friend had had her share of heartbreaks in the past too. But she knew that she would have to tell her the truth soon about what exactly was going on between her and Grayson.

A part of her knew that the reason she had held off on telling her so far was because Eve knew her so well. Eve had been there when Izzy had kissed her very first boyfriend and declared her undying love for him, right in the middle of the street like a fool. She'd seen Izzy at her worst, when her short-lived marriage had been revealed as a farce, and she'd been right there to pick up the pieces.

But that was another time, she reminded herself. The old Izzy might have been tempted to do something so silly as to imagine a true future with a man like Grayson, simply because he'd given her the very best, most attentive lovemaking she'd ever experienced and made her feel like the most beautiful woman in the world. But the new Izzy knew better than to try to sow the seeds of romance where they would never bloom. The new Izzy was learning to enjoy sex with Grayson for what it was, and to look forward to the life they would create from their passion.

Once she was pregnant, and the physical part of their relationship was done, she would come clean to her best friend. But until then she would keep herself grounded.

When Grayson finally returned from race practice he was already running late for their meeting with Astrid and Luca for lunch at their hotel. When he emerged from his bathroom with wet hair, wearing a simple gold-coloured polo shirt and loose ivory trousers, Izzy fought not to stare.

He started to update her on how the new car they were testing was working out on the track, stopping himself when he began to throw out terms like *downforce* and *vortices* and obviously noticed her eyes beginning to glaze over a little.

Then he asked about her work, and she realised that he never glazed over when she talked about her designs. In fact he always remembered specific details, like how she was working on a few proposals for upcoming projects with a big publisher for some jobs that she really hoped she would get. She mentally reminded herself to try to learn a little more about G-forces and tyre compounds.

But mostly the conversation between them felt stilted—as if they were trying to force a friendly vibe that had never truly come easily to either of them in the past. That realisation weighed heavily upon her as they rode side by side in the elevator to Astrid's penthouse suite.

'Falco Roux must be throwing around the big bucks if they can afford to put their PR manager in a place like this,' Izzy said, and whistled as the elevator opened onto a large open-air apartment that had its very own pool built into the terrace.

'Tristan Falco likes to flash his cash, that's for sure,' said Grayson.

'You say that as though you have direct experience?' Izzy raised one brow. She noticed that he looked away quickly at that comment.

'That's one way to put it.' He laughed. 'Another way is to say that he offered me a ridiculous amount of money to cancel my retirement and accept another two-year contract with the team.'

Izzy froze at the realisation that his retirement might possibly not be the permanent thing she'd thought it was. 'That seems…a little over the top.'

'That is the perfect phrase to describe Tristan Falco.'

'Were you tempted?' she asked, feigning nonchalance.

He looked away, giving her the briefest glimpse of an expression that confirmed the answer was undoubtedly yes. He'd been tempted to go back to Elite One racing. Maybe he still was.

Their conversation was interrupted by the fast thump of feet and a loud screech as Luca caught sight of them from his position in the pool and launched himself away from his mother, climbing out and run-

ning straight for them, leaving a river of water in his
wake along the non-slip terrace tiles.

Grayson caught the youngster as he came barrelling into his legs, not seeming to mind that he became
instantly soaked in the process. Luca grinned, then
caught sight of Izzy and frowned.

'You're probably a little surprised to see me here,
eh?' Izzy said softly, taking care to keep just a little
distance between herself and the boy, in case he felt
overwhelmed by her sudden reappearance.

In the end, she needn't have bothered being careful at all, for Luca launched himself bodily from his
uncle's arms and collapsed directly against her chest.
She buried her face in the boy's soft, springy curls
and inhaled his familiar baby shampoo scent.

The lump in her throat turned into a full-blown
rock that she could no longer hold down, and Grayson met her gaze just as a single tear escaped onto
her cheek. He reached out, wiping the tear away with
a look so sincere it melted her heart anew.

Astrid appeared from the kitchen, dressed casu-
ally in jeans and a T-shirt. 'Luca Lewis—what did I
tell you about launching yourself at people like that?
You are not a rocket.'

The little boy answered his mother by launching
himself once again, this time onto the floor, before
pulling on Grayson's hand and urging him out towards the pool he had just emerged from. Grayson
chuckled, shucking off his outer clothes before performing a very impressive cannonball into the water.

Astrid sighed heavily. 'There's no hope of getting him out of there now.'

'Are you talking about the overexcited little boy... or Luca?'

They both laughed at the joke, and Astrid guided her into the modern living area, where she had prepared a table full of finger foods and refreshments.

'I thought the baby years were hard... Nothing could have prepared me for the ferocious fours and fives.'

'Ah, yes, the ferocious fours and fives.' Izzy smiled. 'Not to be undersold by the fury of the terrible twos and torturous threes.'

'He couldn't read when he was three. But now I get sternly worded letters when I displease him.'

'He's reading and writing already?'

Astrid looked out towards the pool, a serious expression momentarily tightening her usually neutral features. 'He reads and writes, but he doesn't talk much yet. His teacher wants us to go for another assessment.'

Izzy looked to where the little boy had emerged from the pool and was taking another running jump back in. The toddler version of Luca she'd known had always been very high-energy, fiercely intelligent and wise beyond his years, but equally prone to challenging moments that had at times felt like a little more than the average toddler tantrums. She had noticed the quirky behaviours that Astrid had mentioned, and she could see how they might stand in his way in the more formal setting of a seated classroom.

AMANDA CINELLI 163

'And how are you feeling about that?' she asked, taking a seat beside her former boss in the way she had often done before in the evenings after Luca's bedtime, when they were both free to relax. They had forged a tentative friendship during those evening conversations, she recalled. That was one of the things she had missed most of all.

'Truthfully? I'm feeling thoroughly out of my depth.' Astrid sighed. 'But I'd do anything if it meant helping him.'

'That's exactly what I would expect you to say.' Izzy smiled. 'He's a great kid, and he's very lucky to have a wonderful mother who is ready to do whatever he needs to thrive.'

'You always did know exactly what to say. So, this thing with Grayson... Am I correct in saying that it feels...serious?'

Guilt churned in Izzy's stomach. It just didn't feel right, keeping Grayson's closest friend out of the loop—not when they planned to have Astrid be a part of their baby's life too.

Before she knew it, she found herself talking. She told Astrid the truth—or at least a pared back version of the truth. That she and Grayson had decided to have a baby together, and co-parent platonically, and this 'relationship' was simply a ruse to set the stage for safety from the press once they'd actually brought a child into the mix.

A tense silence followed, until Astrid began to chuckle softly.

'God, I bet he actually believes that it's fake too.'

Astrid took a long sip of her wine and looked out towards the pool. 'Let me tell you one thing I know for certain about Grayson Koh. The man is the worst actor I have ever met.'

Izzy sat up a little straighter. 'But it's the truth. We came here specifically to pretend we're dating. It's part of our arrangement.'

'So you're telling me there have been no sparks between you while you actively aim to create a child in the traditional sense?' Astrid raised a brow, smiling widely when Izzy avoided her knowing gaze. 'That's exactly what I thought.'

'We have good chemistry, sure. But that's not enough.'

'There is more than chemistry between you two. I saw the way he looked at you from the moment you started working for me. When he told me not to renew your contract, to guide you instead in pursuit of your illustration talents... I don't know why I didn't make sure that was what you wanted before I let you go. He seemed so certain it was what you needed. Believe me, I was furious when he finally admitted to me that he'd wanted to be free to pursue you.'

Izzy was shocked. 'He said that?'

Astrid nodded. 'Izzy, he was smitten, for goodness' sake. You should have seen the look on his face when he found out you were going to Bali with Julian. He even drove to the marina to try and stop you... But you should probably be hearing all this from him.'

Izzy tried to keep a straight face when Luca and Grayson came barrelling into the room before she could press Astrid for more details. She remained calm as they all sat together to eat, but inside her mind was a riot of emotion.

Had he really wanted to stop her going that day she'd left with Julian? Had he really stopped Astrid renewing her contract as some kind of misguided way to give them a chance at being together? It had still been a truly inappropriate move, but knowing he hadn't actually set out to have her fired because he didn't like or approve of her...

She wondered what else she had assumed wrongly about him.

Playing the role of Grayson Koh's adoring girlfriend came a little too easily to her, Izzy discovered as she spent yet another day on the arm of the most charming and attentive boyfriend on the planet.

They had started their day at the official Legends racing weekend launch, where Grayson and a panel of other drivers talked about the goals of the historic event, as well as the personal charities they were supporting. It turned out that Grayson's charity of choice, the Boost Academy, was one that he had started himself years ago, to combat inequality in motorsport.

She could feel his passion as he outlined the many issues that stood in the way of true equality in Elite One, focusing on the costs involved for aspiring racers and how many talented young people were forced to walk away from their dreams due to significant financial barriers and discrimination.

She knew that had very nearly been Grayson's own

experience, and the price he had wound up paying to get his place on the grid was significant. To think that he was purposefully paying that forward by giving others the chance to succeed without any expectation of repayment brought a tear to her eye. She found herself with a newfound understanding of this man who had been doing so much for a very long time with no expectation of praise.

After the launch event they attended a youth race run by the Boost Academy, followed by a lunch where Izzy met a whole host of students past and present who had already benefited from the globally run academy's tutelage and efforts. She watched Grayson laugh and joke with the young drivers, each of whom looked at him with complete awe and admiration, and she could see once again how easy he was around children.

For a man nicknamed the Golden Lion, effortlessly dominant both off the track and on it, he immediately turned into a playful pussycat around youngsters. He had a gentle side that he rarely showed in public, so driven was he to win all the time and to hold his cards close to his chest whilst he did so. But he had always shown it around her, she realised. Even when she'd been his godson's nanny and he had been trying to ignore her.

She had contemplated asking him about what Astrid had divulged the day before, but she wasn't quite sure how to word it.

Hey, Grayson, did you plan to pursue things with

*me before I ruined everything and eloped with your
best friend?*

Even if he had been interested in her back then, she
knew it would only ever have been for a brief fling, to
explore the physical attraction between them. Grayson didn't do relationships, and he most definitely
didn't do commitment and before her disastrous marriage that had been all she'd ever wanted.

Still, being the main focus of Grayson's magneti-
cally charming attentions throughout the day was fast
taking its toll, and she was increasingly having to remind herself that this was all an act. He touched her
at almost every moment, and when he wasn't touching her he was looking at her with that dark, brooding gaze of his.

To any onlookers he'd certainly appear besotted.
But of course Izzy knew that he wasn't holding her
hand under the table and whispering terrible jokes
into her ear because he wanted to. He was simply
playing his part—just as she was.

When the lunch wound to a close, and they'd
waved goodbye to the Boost Academy management
team, she contemplated faking a headache, just so
that she could hide in her bedroom for the rest of the
night and catch her breath.

But Grayson, completely oblivious to her inner
turmoil, announced that he had taken the afternoon
off so that they could do some sightseeing.

With two pairs of dark sunglasses and a discreet
guard trailing them a few paces behind, they walked
the footpath along the banks of the bay with ease,

while Izzy tried desperately to focus on the sights and not the man beside her.

The area around the Marina Bay racetrack boasted views of the most famous sights in Singapore, including the Supertree grove in the gardens by the bay. From a distance, in the afternoon sun, she thought the structures weren't quite as imposing as the pictures she'd viewed online.

'The light show is truly spectacular,' Grayson told her. 'But I'm sure you've seen that before.'

'It was one of the few things I missed out on, actually. Luca was always in bed by that time.' She looked towards the opposite side of the bay, where the grove of manmade trees stood tall. She was not quite ready to give up their time alone just yet. 'Do you think we could stay to watch it?'

'I'm sorry, we have dinner with the Verdant team, followed by another prominent sponsor event.' He winced.

Izzy quickly brushed off her suggestion, easing them away from the subject by asking questions about the Singapore Merlion as they walked towards the famous statue that stood watch over the bay.

Grayson played tour guide as they walked, pointing out small details about the buildings and bridges they passed as only a local could. She loved every small snippet he shared about growing up here, storing away each tiny nugget of information about his childhood as though it might prove useful in understanding the man he was now.

They walked until her feet ached and her stom-

ach began to rumble, and Grayson finally suggested
they stop to eat at one of his favourite places in the
city, a street food centre in the central business district, which boasted stall after stall of authentic fare.

He closed his eyes as he ate, and the word he
growled was one she'd heard often since arriving.
It had thus far evaded her attempts at learning some
simplified Mandarin basics from an audio app on
her phone.

'Does that mean it's tasty?' she asked, noting how
the corner of his mouth rose a little at her question.

'*Shiok?* It's usually used when food is good.' He
reached over, stealing a dumpling from her plate with
a smirk. 'But it's also kind of a catch-all word for
something pleasurable. Winning a race can be *shiok*,
just as a great kiss can be.'

His eyes met hers across the table with meaning,
and she felt a blush creep up from her chest all the
way to her eyebrows as she murmured, 'Seeing the
city with you today was also *shiok*.'

'I'm glad.' He smiled, his hand reaching to cover
hers on the small white table.

All around them voices hummed, and she was
aware of the bodyguard sitting a few tables away, but
for the most part it felt like the most intimate they'd
been with one another since leaving Ireland. Like a
tiny moment of peace. Then there was a flash nearby,
and they both looked up to see a group of teenage
boys approaching them, with phones and Elite One
memorabilia in tow.

More followed, and Grayson apologised to her as

he switched into famous racing driver mode, graciously signing a few items and posing for photos before the bodyguard guided them to a car.

He seemed reserved and brooding as they travelled back to his home, where they had yet another quick turnaround to get ready for the evening events. She knew that his schedule was booked up for the next couple of nights, and then she was scheduled to return to Ireland, but she didn't mind. She was pretty sure he'd rescheduled his day today, to go sightseeing with her.

But maybe the simmering tension between them was all in her mind, and he was quietly relieved that they hadn't been physical since that one night in Ireland? Maybe he had already begun to regret blurring those lines?

She was here to make things easier for both of them in the long run, and yet it felt as if with every moment they spent together she was only complicating things more.

CHAPTER TWELVE

GRAYSON LOUNGED ON a low sofa in the hotel suite he'd booked for the night, waiting as the styling team finished performing whatever magic Isabel had asked them to do. She didn't need magic. Truthfully, he would have been happy having her on his arm in her jeans and black boots if it meant having her smile in his direction again.

She'd been different these last few days, since they'd left Ireland. Sure, his schedule was hectic, and he hadn't made her very comfortable, considering most of their time in public had been spent with him taking every possible chance to touch her and play the adoring boyfriend.

The press adored their fairy-tale love story. Astrid had made a point of telling him that every moment she could. Both he and the Legends event had been trending on social media for three days in a row. For a man who had given so little of himself to the public over the past twenty years, in an effort to shield his supposed deficits, it appeared this more human side of him was infinitely more saleable.

He'd been inundated with requests for and interest in the new Verdant models, and also in him—including a documentary proposal from a major television company. Unveiling the real Grayson Koh beneath his mask of indifference was apparently a big sell in the motorsport world. More of a sell than his shield of ruthless cool had ever been. And he had Isabel to thank for that revelation.

It was the greatest irony, though, that showing the real him to the world meant being fake with the one person whose attention he craved more than any other.

If he had thought that having Isabel in his bed had been torture, it was nothing compared to playing her loving, attentive partner over these past few days. It hadn't been hard at all to appear infatuated with her as they'd attended the various sponsors' events and played tourist around the city in between. But in private she seemed cool, and even a little distant at times, retreating to her room to work on her latest commissions and retiring to bed early.

His plan to seduce her back into his bed seemed to have been foiled at every turn, between his hectic schedule and her determination to hold him at a distance. But this evening's Legends gala ball at the iconic Marina Bay Hotel was to be the penultimate event of the week, followed only by the big race tomorrow night.

He had spent most of today practising, and completing the qualifying laps that would decide everyone's starting position on the grid. It had felt so natural, sliding back into the driver's cockpit, his racing suit and gloves fitting him like a second skin as he'd gripped the wheel in his hands. But even after he had qualified in pole position, surrounded by the comforting sight of his old Falco Roux crew, all he'd been able to think about was returning to Isabel.

She consumed his thoughts—much as she had in that first year, when he'd been unable to stop himself from seeking her out. For a man who'd always prided himself on control and discipline, he'd been unable to resist the lure of even the briefest stolen snapshot of time in her presence.

The problem was, as he'd learned then and as he still knew to be true now, the more time with her he allowed himself, the more he craved. It was a dangerous thing, allowing himself the illusion of having her as his own.

The sound of wheeled cases and clothes racks moved along the hall as the styling team appeared in a flurry of chatter, and Grayson thanked them all before they hurried on to their next appointments. When he turned back, Isabel stood in the centre of the room, looking like every filthy fantasy he'd ever had come to life.

The rich teal-coloured concoction of shimmering fabric hugged her hourglass curves like a second skin, showcasing her ample breasts with a plunging neckline. But his favourite part was the deep slit on one side of the skirt that went up to mid-thigh.

He didn't speak for a long moment, simply looking

his fill as his heart…and other parts of his anatomy… threatened to burst through his tuxedo.

'I'm guessing this is a good silence?' she asked, giving him a slow twirl that showed off the low back of her dress.

'This is a breathtaking, awestruck, give-me-a-moment-to-drink-you-in kind of silence,' he said, fighting off the wave of nerves that had suddenly made him feel tongue-tied.

She looked radiant, but the smile on her face was what had struck him speechless. It was the kind of smile she'd given him long ago, when they had first met.

The gown suited her to perfection. It was sexy, and edgy, and the rich tone complemented the colours of the delicate tattoos that adorned her back. He'd bet she'd chosen to wear her hair up in a sleek ponytail style for exactly that reason.

'You're extra charming this evening.' She smiled, walking beside him towards the floor-length mirrors that bracketed the private elevator. 'You know what I'm going to ask for right now, though, don't you?' She smirked.

Please, please let it be something X-rated.

'What?' he asked, his throat dry, and she popped one curvaceous hip, revealing the gloriously thick length of one pale thigh.

'Let's take a selfie together!' She waved her phone, positioning them both at a flattering angle in front of the mirror and fussing as she angled her camera towards their reflection.

'You know, technically, a selfie is when the camera is pointed towards—'

She pressed one artfully manicured fingertip to his lips. 'Hush with your cranky technicalities. Do as you're told and give me that million-dollar smoulder of yours.'

He did as he was told, facing their reflection and trying not to linger on the sight of them both side by side, his midnight-blue tuxedo jacket acting as the perfect partner to her gown. They looked good together. Too good. They looked as if they fitted perfectly.

He tried to ignore the tightness in his stomach as they stepped into the plush golden interior of the lift while Izzy excitedly tapped on her phone screen and mumbled something about Astrid getting her money's worth this week.

He wanted nothing more than to touch her again. To have her touch him for real. But outside of the few stolen caresses he'd managed during their public appearances, neither of them had made that first move. Their agreement still stood, and it wouldn't be long before she would be back in his bed once more. But it wasn't enough. He was beginning to realise that it probably never would be.

He wanted what they'd had for that brief window of time in her little cottage, when she'd fallen asleep in his arms and he had lain awake, listening to the rain fall outside the windows. That night, much like this one, he'd been awash with a riot of emotions he'd had no idea how to begin untangling. Perhaps that was why, when she had suggested they pretend to be a couple and yet refrain from any repeat rule-breaking, he hadn't contradicted her. Because the alternative was telling her that he wanted her to desire him—not just for their agreement but for *him*.

More and more he found himself dwelling on how things would be when she finally fell pregnant and they moved on to the platonic co-parenting phase of their contract.

Even entertaining the idea of being platonic with her… It made rage and loss build in his gut. He wasn't good enough to have her—he knew that. But what if at some point in the near future someone else decided that they were?

She'd said that she would never have dated again and had children the traditional way, but life could be unpredictable. In taking himself out of the running, he was leaving her out in the open for anyone else to snatch up.

And that was completely unacceptable.

He couldn't simplify it or brush it off by thinking if he couldn't have her no one could. No. He was the kind of selfish bastard who simply wanted her all for himself, and he was fast running out of ways to talk himself out of it.

As though sensing the dangerous nature of his thoughts, Isabel took a tiny step backwards, putting even more distance between them. His eyes narrowed on her. On impulse, he reached out and pressed the emergency stop button. The floor beneath them vibrated as they came to a smooth stop, and a small blinking red light came on above their heads.

'What are you doing?' She frowned, reaching to remove his hand.

'Being spontaneous.'

'But we're already running late,' she said, her eyes widening as he stepped closer, bracketing her with his arms on either side of her head.

'Our captive audience can wait,' he growled, his eyes not leaving hers. 'I cannot.'

Her mouth dropped open a little, and the delicate pulse at her throat was visibly thrumming as she looked down, as if realising just how little space separated them.

He catalogued all these reactions, running them against what he already knew of her tells, and came to one glorious deduction. In this moment she was not pretending to be indifferent to him, and nor was she afraid. Far from it. She was…excited. There was no crowd here to appease. No audience. Just as he needed it to be if he was to say these next words aloud.

'You're running from me again, Isabel,' he said softly, reaching up to cup her jaw with one hand.

She inhaled sharply at his touch, but this time she did not look away. Thank goodness. Because he didn't think he could bear it. He needed her eyes on him. Her hands on him.

'I'm right here…' she breathed.

'You are…and we're going to talk.' He forced himself not to pounce, not to claim her as he craved. Not before she said the words he wanted to hear. 'Be honest with me, Isabel…have you not missed my touch at all?'

She frowned, looking past him. 'Our deal doesn't start up again for another few days. We said we'd keep things normal outside of…those days.'

'*You* said that. I, however, thought I was quite clear on where I stood in that regard. I need you to know that if this had been about what *I* wanted…you would never have left my bed.'

'You don't actually mean that. Not when you have crowds of beautiful half-naked women lusting after you.'

'Ah…you saw the foam party photos.'

He had hated every moment of that ridiculous event, but he had been forced to stand and pose with dancers for the press and various social media influencers as part of his sponsorship commitments for the upcoming race.

'I didn't think this through,' she said. 'This part of your life. I feel like I'm cramping your style.'

'We discussed exclusivity and I stand by my commitments. Not just for our agreement, but because the idea that I'd have any interest in some stranger throwing her clothing at me when I can barely think straight for wanting *you* is laughable. I spent most of my practice session today fantasising about our next window…of how I might convince you to extend it to a week instead of three nights. Maybe even two.'

'I may as well just take up residence in your bed at that rate.'

'Yes,' he said simply, watching her cheeks turn that beautiful shade of pink he loved so much.

He had coveted her blushes, not getting nearly enough of them since they'd begun this ruse.

No longer would he go without them.

'Grayson, what exactly are you saying?' she asked, her voice a small whisper.

'I'm saying yes. Yes to you taking up residence in my bed. No more pretending, Isabel. I'm done with taking these small pieces of you and expecting satisfaction. I crave you and I want it all.'

Her mouth formed the most delicious little O and, damn it, weak as he was, he leaned in and stole her next exhalation of breath with a kiss, before pulling swiftly back. 'Sorry, I couldn't resist. You don't have to answer me right now. I understand that you have your hang-ups—'

Whatever he'd been about to say next was swallowed up by Isabel's perfectly painted red lips as she launched herself at him in a kiss to end all other kisses. She tasted like sweet plums and spice, her tongue sliding against his own without any of the nerves she'd shown before. She was a goddess, and he was utterly at her mercy. Her hands gripped his hair, her soft weight pushing him back against the wall of the elevator, pinning him in place.

'What is this, hmm?' he murmured against her lips.

'This is me answering you,' she said roughly, deepening the kiss until only the sound of their laboured breathing filled the elevator.

The sound of a low beep permeated the air, and it took Grayson a moment to realise that it was coming from the emergency call panel. Placing his finger upon Isabel's lips, he pressed the button and briefly addressed the concierge on the other end.

'Did you seriously just offer that man an inordinate amount of money to give us ten minutes alone in here?' Isabel's husky whisper turned into a gasp as Grayson's lips trailed down the side of her neck.

'Believe me, I'd have asked for two hours if I could.'

He gripped her waist, swapping their positions so that she was pinned and at his mercy. He only had ten minutes, and he didn't intend to waste a single moment with discussion. Without breaking eye contact, he sank down slowly to his knees.

Izzy felt all rational thought leave her as Grayson's strong hands bracketed her thighs and spread her dress wide. A flimsy scrap of lace was all that separated them. She leaned her head back against the elevator wall and silently thanked her stylist for selecting a gown made of some magical kind of ultra-fitted stretch material that required no supportive garments beneath. She didn't think she could have managed a straight face if he'd needed to forcibly extract her from her underwear in order to do whatever it was he had planned.

With one deft flick of his fingers her knickers were in his pocket and his mouth was delving hungrily between her thighs. The act felt both crude and impossibly tender as he framed her sex with one hand, reaching the other up to twine his fingers with hers.

She felt too exposed, too open to him in so many ways. But just when she was about to tell him to stop, he hooked one thumb behind her thigh and raised it to rest upon his strong shoulders. The position was scandalously erotic, and made it utterly impossible for her to hold on to the tiny scrap of control she'd been clinging to any longer. With every sweep of his tongue against her she felt herself tighten, careening down a runway of pleasure that Grayson alone was in charge of.

She was not the one in control here, and she didn't think she truly wanted to be. And that was a revelation.

Trusting him to get her there, to keep her safe in this tiny pocket of time... It gave her a strength and confidence she didn't know she'd been searching for. She clutched at every part of him she could reach—his hair, the nape of his neck. She leaned into his dominant strength and held on for dear life as the strongest orgasm she'd ever experienced crested, sending glorious waves of pleasure through her very core.

Her legs trembled, but Grayson was right there holding her as she came back to her senses, a sinful smile on his lips as he stared up at her.

He was still on his knees, and he made no move to stand right away. He simply held her for a moment, his hands circling her hips and his face pressed against the softness of her stomach. Then he stood, staring down at her with a look of dark possession that sent skitters of excitement and trepidation through her.

In the back of her mind she knew that she was hurtling faster than she had ever anticipated towards falling for this man. Maybe she was fooling herself to think she hadn't already been halfway there from the moment they'd met. She wanted him more than he could know. He'd said he craved her, but he had no idea of the depth of feeling coursing through her in this moment.

'I want you inside me,' she whispered, pulling him close against her.

He shook his head, his fingers smoothing her errant hair away from her face. 'Not yet.'

Not yet? She frowned, wondering what exactly that meant. But of course… Reality returned, and she realised that they still stood in the lift. Probably rapidly approaching the end of their ten-minute window and thus risking discovery. Public indecency was not something taken lightly in this part of the world, and she could hardly believe that they had taken it this far, even with Grayson's assurance of privacy.

'Isabel, look at me,' he commanded, waiting until her gaze met his. 'Don't for a second think that I didn't mean anything I just said. I meant all of it. When I make love to you again, I want complete certainty between us. Do you understand?'

'Yes, I… I think so.'

Her mind was racing, muddled in the aftermath of the destruction he'd just wrought upon her control. Everything was going so fast…but she felt happy. It was slightly terrifying, but she felt as if something truly cataclysmic had occurred in the last ten minutes.

He helped her put her dress to rights, smoothing down the folds all the way to her feet with a tenderness and attention to detail that tightened her chest. He always took care of her, she realised with clarity. From the very beginning he had done all those tiny things that she so often overlooked doing for herself. She had spent so much of her life just surviving that small comforts seemed to bypass her attention completely.

He moved to press the emergency button once more, and the lift began to move again.

Far too soon they had reached the foyer, and the doors opened to reveal them to the crowd of guests and the few select photographers who were allowed to attend.

Grayson took her by the hand, guiding her to where a small gathering of people with familiar faces stood. Nina Roux wore a glamorous red ballgown and was in avid conversation with Astrid, who wore an equally stunning sheath of gold sequinned silk.

'I'm going to leave you for a moment, but I'll be right back,' Grayson said, pressing a kiss to the inside of her wrist before letting her hand drop. 'I just have something I need to do.'

Izzy watched as he moved away, towards the private elevator they'd just exited. 'But, Grayson, where are you—?'

Her words were swallowed by the crowd, and she

could do nothing but watch as the doors of the lift slid shut and he disappeared from her view.

'What on earth is that lovestruck fool up to now?' Astrid mused softly beside her.

Izzy tried not to let her nerves get to her as minutes passed and Grayson didn't reappear. All too soon they were being called into the sprawling event space on the Skydeck, where wildflowers decorated every surface. It felt like walking into an enchanted forest, with the music pumping from the speakers below their feet seeming somehow ethereal.

It wasn't long before she was left on her own on the edge of the balcony as the others scurried off to their duties. They had a purpose here, while she… Well, she tried not to think too negatively about how very small and out of place she felt.

Grayson wasn't lovestruck over her—not really. Was he?

She needed to go and find him and ask him for herself.

Downing the last of her drink, she made her way through the crowd with as much calm and poise as she could muster. She wasn't running away, she told herself. She was running *to* him.

She emerged back into the foyer, the now-empty space feeling cavernous and cold without the throng of guests that had filled it before. But it wasn't empty. A man stood nearby A man with a face she had only ever seen once before, on a day that had left scars on her confidence that she'd fought hard to heal.

Peter Liang. Julian's father.

CHAPTER THIRTEEN

'I HEARD YOU'D found yourself a new target,' the old man croaked, his voice just as thin and reedy as she remembered.

Isabel stood frozen in place, her hand still braced on the handle of the door she'd just come through.

She'd known that by coming here she would have to face the Liang family eventually, but she hadn't been prepared for it tonight. She hadn't been prepared to be alone when it happened, either.

Her words seemed stuck in her throat, her ability to fight back trapped beneath a layer of ice. For all her talk about finding her power and rebuilding her life, she'd still never quite mastered the art of conflict. But here, in this grand hotel, there was nowhere to run without causing a scene. So she decided she had nothing to lose.

She had long thought about what she might say if she ever saw any of her late husband's family again. How she might lay to rest the burden of guilt she had carried over how his life had come to an end. This was her opportunity.

'I had hoped to see you while I was here,' she lied, planting her feet and inhaling a sharp breath. 'If only to tell you how utterly disappointed I am.'

'You're disappointed?' He laughed. 'Is that supposed to make me feel something?'

'Oh, no, I wouldn't say anything is capable of doing that, Mr Liang,' she said neutrally. 'Not a man who treats his children like pawns. Julian may not have been perfect, but he didn't deserve the way you treated him. And as for Grayson...'

The old man smiled, looking over her shoulder. 'Ah, yes, please do champion your new lover to me. Some pretty tears might even earn you some diamonds if you start now.'

Isabel looked behind her to see Grayson emerging from the lift, his expression swiftly tightening into alarm as he realised who was with her.

She vaguely processed the sight of Grayson storming in front of her, his voice tight as the two men began arguing in their native tongue. She had never managed to learn more than a select few words, but judging by the increasingly tight line of Peter Liang's lips whatever Grayson had to say was not pleasant.

Not a moment too soon, Grayson turned to her and ushered her back through the doors to where the gala was now in full swing. Humid fragrant air filled her lungs and the music chased away all the unpleasantness of the past few moments.

'Are you okay?' Grayson asked softly, his nostrils still slightly flared with anger.

'I'm fine. I wanted to speak with him...to say how

I felt. And I did.' She exhaled a long, steady breath. 'The real question is are *you* okay? That sounded like it got pretty heated.'

'That is not how I planned for tonight to go. I didn't think he would be attending, considering his own team has gone bust and he's had to pull all his funding from the Singapore Elite One race. That's what we argued over, mostly.'

'And about me?' she offered.

'I don't care what he thinks about me, and I told him as much. But I told him that if he so much as attempts to upset you ever again, I will buy everything he owns from under him.'

Izzy tried not to be shocked at the vehemence in his voice, but she could see that he meant it. She could see that he would defend her in this against anyone who dared to draw attention to their mismatched pairing. But deep down a small part of her wondered if that was right. If perhaps they would always be up against all those comments that painted her as an opportunist.

Her uncertainty followed her as Grayson was called away to attend to his duties as one of the hosts. But before he walked away he kissed her, right in the middle of the dance floor, much to the delight of the crowd around them. As she smiled up at him on stage she knew she couldn't deny it any longer. She was deeply, madly in love with this gorgeous man.

But she felt as if she'd decided to stay safe, only to climb back out onto the precipice all over again now. She knew that Grayson would never truly love her as she needed him to, nor want to be a family with her for real, so stepping into this in-between life with him was dangerous to her heart. As was getting close to his friends.

Because that was what they had always been, wasn't it?

His friends. Not hers.

Sure, she had Astrid and Luca now, but what if they decided she wasn't good enough for Grayson and abandoned her? Only it wouldn't just be her— it would be an innocent baby in the middle of it all. She knew how intoxicating it felt to be enfolded into their big racing family, and how cold it had been in contrast once she'd been cast out.

Logically, she knew she was being irrational, but she couldn't stop those feelings from bubbling up to the surface like oil, coating all her fragile hope with fear. She could hardly smile, and her limbs felt numb as Grayson began to give a speech about the various charities that would benefit from the Legends race.

He was effortlessly charming, and she knew that while he might technically be retired, this would always be his world. He belonged here. But she didn't, and she had been fooling herself to think that their great chemistry in bed was enough to change that.

She had been prepared to have a baby with him— to co-parent and have nice, tidy boundaries. Control. Temporary visits she could walk away from when their time was up. But now she'd gone and fallen for him and everything had changed. She'd already begun to lose herself in the illusion that this fantasy might have a happy ending, when he had always been up-front about the fact that it never could. He wasn't a happily-ever-after kind of guy.

Just pull it off.

She bit down hard on her lip, repeating the mantra that had always got her through much worse times than this. With Astrid by her side, she had to turn her face away and choke down her tears. She knew she couldn't stay here. She had always known. And there was no sense in prolonging the inevitable because it would only hurt more.

She had to pull off the sticking plaster—fast and clean.

She had hoped that once the formal part of the gala had drawn to a close she might be able to convince Grayson to take her back to the suite. She knew that this was a conversation best had in private. But he'd suggested that they take a walk, said that he had something special planned…

She was powerless to resist the chance for even one more hour spent living in the fantasy.

She wasn't entirely sure what she planned to say to him—only knew she had to tell him that they couldn't do this for real. She had no guarantee that he would want to keep to their arrangement either. She was risking so much… But the alternative was more than she could bear.

Everything felt like too much, and with every step that she took, following him across the narrow bridge that separated the hotel from the beautifully ornate gardens that made Singapore so very famous, she felt her body grow tight with trepidation. They were going into the gardens they hadn't been able to stay in before, because of all his commitments.

'Surely this place is closed at this time of the night?' she asked, as Grayson guided her along a polished stone pathway towards the world-famous Supertrees Grove.

'I made a special request. It pays to be the country's only championship-winning Elite One driver sometimes.' He winked, looking lighter than she had seen him all week.

'This is beautiful,' she said, looking up to where the man-made 'trees' were lit up in pinks and yellows and purples. The sky seemed to glitter around them, the colours touching her skin and illuminating the fabric of her dress like a tapestry.

When she looked back at Grayson, he had a strange expression on his face.

'You've been happy with me this past week here, yes?' he asked. 'I hope that I've come to know you well enough to know when you're happy.'

'Of course I've been happy.' She looked out at the skyline, at the beauty of their surroundings, but still inside she felt a chasm open within her. 'Grayson... I think that sometimes we tend to idealise situations because we really want them to work...'

'Are we talking about me here, or you?' he asked.

'Maybe just me...' She swallowed past the lump in her throat. 'I don't know... All I know is that we are far too different. We have very different visions of our future, which is why we entered into this agreement. We both agreed that our situation would work best from a distance.'

'But what if it isn't best?' he said softly, reaching out to take her hand in his. 'You look so beautiful right now. But your beauty isn't the only thing that has me in your thrall. It's everything about you...'

She shook her head, pain lancing her chest with every word. 'Grayson, I—'

'Please, just let me get this out first. Just let me...'

He inhaled a sharp breath, reaching into his tuxedo pocket and pulling out a small velvet box. Time slowed as he met her eyes with a heart-melting smile, popping the box open to reveal a glittering diamond ring.

'I said I wanted you to be certain of what I want the next time we made love, so I decided that I'd make myself as clear as possible.'

Izzy watched with a mixture of awe and horror as Grayson dropped to his knees before her for the second time that evening.

Grayson stared up at Isabel's shocked face and instantly knew that he had made a mistake.

Silence fell between them, but still he remained frozen in place, hoping that she was simply taken by surprise. That any moment now she would laugh and fall into his arms, shouting the one little word he needed to hear.

But she didn't laugh. Nor did she speak.

When he looked closer, he realised that her bottom lip was quivering and she was beginning to cry. Somewhere along the line he had misread the signs, overlooked something crucial, and now they were careening off-track.

He stood up quickly, gripping her hands in his, hating how cold they felt.

'This went differently in my mind… I won't lie.' He'd aimed for a joking tone, but his voice came out just as strained as he felt.

Still she didn't respond.

'Isabel, I mean this. I want us to be married. I want us to raise our child together, as a family.'

She closed her eyes, shaking her head softly, as though his words were breaking her heart—which made absolutely no sense.

'Damn you,' she whispered, the words escaping on a hiss of pain. 'I was prepared to do all this alone, and then you walked into my life and made me start to hope.'

'Hope is good,' he urged.

'Not when the thing I had been hoping for was…' She opened her eyes. 'You told me how you felt about marriage once—or have you forgotten? You told me years ago that the only way you could abide the institution would be if there were no emotions involved. "Just sex and finances." I believe those were your words. You've told me you crave me…but I've done something so much worse. I've somehow gone and fallen in love with you.'

He felt her admission like a punch to the chest, stopping his heart and then starting it up all over again. He held her tighter to him, refusing to let her go. She wouldn't run from him this time—not when he had waited years to have her.

But then he felt the certainty within him that he deserved such a glorious gift wane—just for a split second. He froze, and time stretched out as her eyelashes fluttered and lowered to a close.

One moment of hesitation—that was all it took for Isabel's trust in him to vanish completely. He saw it in her face as her expression crumpled.

She tried to pull herself free from his grip but he held on tight, gathering her more closely into the circle of his arms. The lights that sparkled pink and purple above them now shimmered upon the tears that fell freely down her cheeks. Tears that somehow he had caused, with his inability to trust in himself.

But the right words wouldn't quite come.

'I… I adore you, Isabel,' he stammered. 'You must know that.'

'Must I?' She sniffed, successfully pulling away from him this time. 'Because from what you've told me, you've only ever seen marriage as a cold, meaningless union. The fact that you've decided to pursue it with me tells me everything I need to know.'

He closed his eyes, cursing his past self for being so cynical and his present self for being so damned obtuse. 'There is nothing cold about how I feel for you.'

'I know. And that makes it so much worse. Marrying each other would be a huge risk, Grayson. And it's simply not one I'm prepared to take. Not when we can stick to our original plan and avoid the drama and the heartbreak.'

'Maybe I've gone about this the wrong way... We should go home and talk.'

'It's not my home, Grayson. I have my home. I had everything in my life settled just the way I wanted it. And then...'

'I came along and ruined everything?' he suggested.

'Don't put words in my mouth. I am not saying that our time together has been a waste. Or that it has had no effect on me, or that I wish it had never happened. I am unbelievably happy that it happened, and that I got to experience what it feels like to be the focus of your attention.'

'But that's how it can be always. That's how it will be if you just give us a chance.'

She shook her head sadly. 'I can't marry you, Grayson.'

He felt her words like a weight in his chest as she slowly took a step backwards. Her jaw was tight, her lips set in a grim line, and he could see that she truly believed the words she spoke.

On some primal level he wanted nothing more than to throw her over his shoulder and take her back to his bed, where he would work on convincing her otherwise. He would show her just how very alike they were in all the ways that mattered, and just how wonderful their life together could be if she gave in.

But another part of him asked if he wanted what was best for her or if he simply wanted her at all costs. If he convinced her to marry him, to stay with him here in Singapore, she'd have to sell her house and change all her plans just to fit in with his world. Because that was how it would have to be. He had a busy lifestyle that took him all around the world, and his plans frequently changed at the last minute. He was often exhausted, and he barely had time for social occasions, never mind the demands of being a part of a committed relationship. Wasn't that why his last one had failed?

Did he want her badly enough to force her into his world if he couldn't make her happy? Was that love? Or would the true act of love be letting her go and giving her the gift of the secure home and quiet life-style that she could only have without him?

CHAPTER FOURTEEN

GRAYSON COMPLETED HIS warm-up laps, trying and failing to feel the familiar pre-race hum of anticipation in his veins. Drivers on the track often compared a good relationship with their car to sex. Compatibility, connection, trust, feel... A poor feel for a car could have the best driver sliding around the track like a rookie, but a good feel...it made everything seamless. Hyperfocus kicked in and you felt unstoppable, as if you were flying on land.

Making love with Isabel was like that.

Seamless. Right.

So much for his pre-race calming rituals. He had never felt as wound up in his entire career, and it had nothing to do with the race and everything to do with the fact that Isabel was running late and likely wouldn't make it to the garage before the race began. Also, she had called Astrid to pass along that message and not him. Sure, the garage was technically a mobile-phone-free area, but did she know that?

He tried not to let his mind run wild with the possibility that she had made her decision to end things and was already on her way back to Ireland. After a few hours of fitful sleep he'd left the hotel before she woke—a necessity, to avoid sliding into bed alongside her to rehash his points from the night before. He knew her well enough by now to realise that would only send her running away faster.

The more he thought over his rash proposal, the more he realised what a mistake it had been. He had been selfish, wanting to keep her with him by any means possible. He had pushed away her worries that they were too different, but now he'd calmed down he could see things from her perspective. She had told him how important it was for her to lay down roots and commit herself to parenthood, and he had told her that he wasn't cut out to be a full-time family man. That his career was number one.

Was it any wonder she doubted him?

He closed his eyes, wondering how on earth he had got everything so wrong. She loved him. She trusted him with the role of her child's father, but not with her heart. And why would she trust him with that most precious commodity when he had all but told her he would never love her?

He'd believed the words when he'd originally spoken them, not seeing a world where he would ever willingly enter into marriage with romantic notions. He could never have predicted the speed with which he would become a lovesick fool for a chaotic blonde tornado full of colour and joy.

But then again, wasn't that why he had sent her running away all those years ago? Hadn't he admitted that he felt that connection and pushed her away because of it?

He slammed his hand down hard on the wheel, watching as the engineers moved off the track.

'Grayson, she's here.'

It took him a moment to realise that one of his engineers was alerting him to Isabel's arrival, as he'd requested.

'Put her on.'

A small commotion could be heard amongst the familiar sounds of equipment and voices and the music pulsing for the crowds as they awaited the race to begin. Thankfully his team didn't question their driver's very unconventional request, and within thirty seconds, Isabel's breathless and slightly awkward *'Hey...'* graced his ears.

'Hey, yourself,' he said, feeling the tension of the silence between them for a breath. He despised this tension, and if he'd been with her in person he'd have done his best to dispel it as quickly as possible. As it was, he could only show her how he felt. 'Can you see me on the monitor?'

'Is that...is that one of my designs on your helmet?'

'Yes. I had it made years ago.' He smiled at the memory of finding a drawing she'd made for Luca left at the Falco Roux garage one time. 'I needed it with me today. I should have known back then that things were never going to be simple between us. I know you're surrounded by musty old men right now, who are probably highly entertained by all this, but I need you to know that I'm sorry I tried to rush things. But I'm not sorry for what I said last night. I meant every word.'

A voice cut across them as comms came in from various officials, announcing the clearing of the track.

He cleared his throat, realising his time was up, but needing to know that when this race was done she would be right there waiting for him. 'Sounds like I've got to go.'

'Yes.'

'You said that you can't marry me, and I will try and respect that… But you can't ask me to stop hoping that I haven't completely messed this up. I would walk away from this race right now just to hear you tell me you love me again.'

'Grayson, I… I'll be here waiting for you. I promise.'

It wasn't quite the profession of love he'd hoped for, but it was a start. Maybe that was what they needed— a fresh start.

The sound of the engines all around him permeated his thoughts, reminding him that he was here to perform a job. He had a charity relying on him, and fans waiting for the dramatic show he always delivered. He focused on his breathing as he felt the familiar thrum of his engine and heard the shouts of the crowd.

He wouldn't let Isabel return to Ireland without pleading his case one more time, but first he would focus on winning this race.

Izzy swore she could feel the heat of more than a dozen gazes focused on her as she took a step back

from the pit wall and shakily handed the headset back
to the head engineer.

The man had a rosy tint to his cheeks as he gave
her a knowing nod. The rest of the team purposefully
gave her some space, and got back to work commu-
nicating with Grayson as his engine roared to life
and the race began.

She made a beeline for the bathroom at the rear
of the garage, not really caring where she ended up,
just needing to be alone for a moment. Knowing that
Grayson would be driving at high speed in rainy conditions had already had her nerves in a knot as she'd
rushed to make it for the start of the race, but after
that conversation her stomach was in a knot for a
whole other reason.

Was she running away?

If she knew one thing about herself, it was that
she felt the most discomfort when she was making
connections with people. She didn't need a degree in
psychology to know why. A lifetime of inconsistency
and let-downs and abandonment had led to her devel-
oping a thicker skin than most. Perhaps even a kind
of armour that she encased herself within. Had she
made a mistake, disregarding his proposal the night
before? Had she projected feelings onto him that were
more hers than his?

She was so tired of holding herself at a distance
all the time. It didn't feel like protection or comfort.
Around Grayson she felt in every second she was with
him that she was holding up a weight that he was already helping her to support. When she needed him,

he was there. And when he messed up he tried to make it better by *being* better, not just making empty promises. He sought her out, and he saw her far too clearly...over-defensiveness and all.

Even after she had rejected his beautiful proposal the night before and practically run from him, hiding in her bedroom all night in floods of tears, he had still worried about her when she hadn't turned up. He had been sitting in the cockpit of an Elite One racing car, his favourite place in the whole world after months away from it, and he'd wanted to talk to *her*.

She stared at her own reflection in the bathroom mirror, feeling a bubble of emotion burst upwards through her chest. But it wasn't a sob that escaped her lips, it was a laugh. A laugh at her own foolishness and at his ridiculously romantic confession to her and the entire pit team. The man had no shame and arrogance to burn...it was what she loved most about him.

There was very little about him that she didn't like—that was what had always drawn her to him. Even though she knew his reputation on the track and in the tabloids, the Grayson that she had spent those snapshots of time with had been everything she had ever wanted. As if someone had drawn together everything that she might need in a partner to feel whole and wrapped it up in one gorgeous, brooding package.

She took a deep breath, and then another, hardly believing the direction her thoughts had taken. It felt

like whiplash—she had been so certain the night before, so steadfast in her reasoning that they would
never work as a couple.

The rain had never been this bad on the Singapore
track in all the years Grayson had driven it. It fell in
heavy sheets, and the track glistened like ice as he
worked to keep his pace. His skill on a wet track was
unmatched, and if this had been a usual Elite One
race such conditions would have likely given him
full advantage.

But this wasn't a usual race—in so many ways.
From the moment he had set off, after lights out, part
of his mind had continued to wander to the woman
he knew stood in the garage, watching him.

He was keenly aware of that fact as he took each
corner at speed, as he felt the give of his tyres on the
track, every time edging closer to losing control, just
on the precipice. And as he ended his first lap, knowing he still had countless more to go, he knew that
at some point over the past weeks with Isabel he had
been irrevocably changed.

He turned another hairpin bend just at the moment
when the backmarker hit the wall and careened into
a full spinning flip, coming towards him...

All he could think about was how sorry he was
not to have told her he loved her.

CHAPTER FIFTEEN

Izzy FELT THE energy in the garage shift even before the sound of screeching tyres echoed in the distance. Everyone froze in place as they watched the action unfold on the multiple monitors that were spread across the wall. Cars spinning in stunning HD focus filled each screen at different angles, multiplying the sick knot twisting in her solar plexus.

All she could tell was that one driver had taken a turn too fast, lost control, and created an incident that had sent multiple other cars spinning. She struggled to make out each of the vehicles in the rain, trying to see which driver's helmet was the same colour as Grayson's. Which one had *his* name emblazoned on the side panel.

She was nudged to the side-lines as members of the Falco Roux team began to confer in multiple languages she couldn't understand, watching and analysing as much as they could. She knew that this was their job, that unlike her they actually knew what to look for to see if their teammate was okay. They had headsets connecting them to Grayson's car directly, as well as to the marshals and stewards on the scene...

Heels sounded down the corridor at the rear of the garage and she had never felt such relief flood through her as when she saw Astrid's frantic form burst through the doorway. She had been upstairs, schmoozing with upper management and the sponsors of the event. Izzy had been invited to sit up there as well, but she had told Astrid she needed to be down here to support Grayson.

Now, she almost laughed out loud at how utterly ridiculous that idea was. She was powerless to do anything at all right now, other than wait and try to keep out of the way.

Astrid didn't speak, simply held her hand. Both of them were looking towards the monitors in a silent plea. After a few moments there was a noticeable exhalation of breath from the professionals in the room. Izzy sat to attention as the team principal announced loudly in English that all the drivers involved in the collision were okay and that both of the Falco Roux drivers were on their way back to the garage while a large amount of debris on the track was cleared.

'We're looking at a restart, everyone,' the team principal told them, and then began listing a barrage of technical instructions that sent everyone into action.

Izzy felt her body go into shutdown after the adrenaline rush, dropping her face into her hands as a few silent sobs burst free from her chest.

He was okay.

She focused on watching the monitor that currently showed a British driver being escorted to an ambulance as he waved a hand to the crowd, to show he was okay. It was no use. She still felt as if her heart was about to thump right out of her chest.

She heard the roar of the Falco Roux cars coming to a stop behind her, but couldn't quite bring herself to stand. She felt foolish because of how utterly shaken she was, compared with these people who were so experienced with all the drama and unpredictability of Elite One.

She looked up to see Grayson's broad figure emerging out of the cockpit of his car.

'What are you doing?' the team principal roared, 'You're in pole position—this isn't the time for a bathroom break, Grayson.'

'It's a restart—they can wait.'

The crew parted as Grayson traversed the length of the garage with no more than a few purposeful strides, the visor of his helmet pulled upwards to reveal the full intensity of his gaze upon one person.

Her.

He looked like a warrior returning from battle as he undid the clasp underneath his helmet and pulled it off. His jet-black hair was wet with the sweat that dripped down along his perfectly chiselled jaw. His mouth was set in a grim line as he came to a stop in front of her, cursing softly under his breath.

'Look at you. You're as white as a sheet.'

His hand rose up to cup her jaw so tenderly, in contrast with the wild expression in his gaze. The team principal once again called for him to return to his car, but Grayson ignored him. His eyes remained fixed on hers in a look so anguished it took her breath away.

'Listen to them,' she said quickly, keenly aware of all the eyes upon them. 'You have a race to finish. Honestly, I'm fine.'

'Are you?' he asked, his eyes seeing far too much as usual. 'Because I'm not.'

'You're hurt?'

She felt a fresh wave of alarm shoot through her as she scanned his body for signs of bleeding, reflexively reaching out a hand to run it along the side of his ribs.

He closed his eyes, inhaling a deep breath at the contact.

'Oh, my God, you *are* hurt.'

She tried to pull her hand back, only to have him pin it in place in the spot directly over his heart.

'Not hurt. But not okay,' he said roughly, his tone so far from the smooth, confident, arrogant voice that he had used over the radio. 'Do you have any idea how many times in my career I've been in a situation like that, or even worse? More than I can count. I'm known for thriving on the chaos. My mind clears to nothing but winning, my reflexes kick in, and I use the adrenaline as fuel. I don't allow myself to feel fear.'

Izzy inhaled a shuddering breath. He had told her before that he rarely felt nerves in the car, but right now his hand shook just a little over hers, and she could feel the frantic thumping of his heart against her fingertips.

'Isabel... I saw that crash happening ahead... coming right at me...and for the first time in my entire career I didn't think about winning. All I could think about was you.' He leaned in, his damp forehead pressing against hers as he fought to get his breathing under control. 'I could see your face so clearly in my mind...and I realised winning meant nothing to me compared to being able to walk back in here to you.'

'This is your *job*, Grayson. I understand the risks and I'm here to cheer you on. Whether it's just for today or if you decide to go back into Elite One. I would never stand in the way of your dream.'

'I know you wouldn't. And I adore you all the more for it. But that's the thing. I don't think this is my dream any more. Only one thing has made me feel right in a long time, and I'm holding her in my arms.'

She closed her eyes, the impact of his words hitting her squarely in the chest. Had anyone ever said anything like that to her in her entire life? Had anyone ever quite literally dropped everything to run to her, just to see that she was okay?

'But if you don't go back to the car you're going to lose the race. You love winning.'

'Nowhere near as much as I love you, Isabel O'Sullivan.' He took her face in his hands, brown eyes blazing bronze with the force of his words. 'I messed up last night. You have no idea how many times I've gone over that proposal in my head and wished that I'd gone about it differently. But once I want something I get tunnel vision…and you have become my entire focus. Not just creating a baby with you… You—yourself. I told you that my career has always been front and centre and always would be… And I truly believed that. I truly believed that I wanted to have a child at a distance, so that it wouldn't have too much of an effect on my vision for motor-sport. My own ego astounds me even now. To think that I could ever have been so utterly blind. And even once I realised that I was falling for you I still held back. I still tried to hold on to what I believed I was, letting you believe that you would only ever get a part of me. But being with you these past few weeks has reawakened all of those old feelings that made me push you away before, simply because they terrified me. I wasn't ready for you then. I was too selfish. I probably still am too selfish…'

'You are the most unselfish man I have ever known,' she told him. 'You have done nothing but make me feel safe and secure and loved…even though I didn't recognise it for what it was. I'm sorry that I tried to push you away.'

'Does that mean that you're done with doing that?'

'I can't promise that I won't feel insecure from time to time—wounds like mine don't really disappear—but I'm ready to try. I've had the dress rehearsal this past week, and now I'm ready to be loved by you for real.'

'Haven't you realised yet? It was always real.'

He gathered her in his arms, his lips claiming hers in a kiss so scorching hot that she heard quite a few whoops and cheers coming from their audience. Grayson pulled back for a second, framing her face with his hands as he looked down at her, love and adoration quite literally beaming from him. Then he turned to his teammate.

'Nina, go and win that race for Falco Roux, like I know you can.'

Nina Roux's eyes shone brightly through the gap in her visor before she gave a single-hand salute and sped out into the pit lane to restart the race.

After that Grayson didn't wait very long, taking her by the hand and practically pulling her through the corridors and paths of the Elite One paddock towards his luxurious private dressing room.

'But Grayson...what about winning?' Izzy asked breathlessly as he slammed the door behind them and began frantically undressing them both.

'You think I'd waste a moment out there when the best prize I've ever won is right here?' He leaned in to capture another scorching kiss.

She paused, smirking. 'If I'm the best prize you've ever won...would that make me your trophy wife?'

'Funny.' He laughed, but then his expression turned serious. 'Have you changed your mind about marrying me? Because I don't have the ring—'

'I don't need a ring, Grayson. I just need you.'

He pulled her into his arms. 'I told myself that you deserved better than the chaotic life I can give you... But while I don't know if I'll ever feel like I truly deserve your love I'm going to take it. And I'm going to do my best to show you how much I love you every single day.'

And then he kissed her again…a kiss filled with the promise of for ever.

EPILOGUE

'IF YOU SLOW down any more we'll be driving back-wards!' Izzy laughed as her husband took yet another hairpin bend in the country road at a snail's pace.

'I'm taking appropriate safety measures for the rain,' he grumbled. 'And for your nausea.'

'My nausea is behaving itself this morning.' She smiled, patting a hand on her still soft belly, where their baby was growing nicely. 'But if we keep going at this pace I may faint from hunger.'

'We have one pitstop to make before we get to brunch,' he said, his jaw ticking again in that terse way it did when he was nervous.

What was he up to?

'I'll push for max speed while we're on the straight here, shall I?' He smirked, flipping the gear shift of the car just the way she liked.

'Copy that, Grayson. Push, push.' She gave him her best Elite One radio voice.

He'd recently made good on his promise to do filthy things to her atop one of the cars in a dark-ened garage after the Brazilian Grand Prix, before taking them home to Ireland for a much-needed winter break. They'd had their first Christmas dinner in her tiny cottage with Eve and her wife Moira and their daughter as their honorary guests.

The rain was coming down more heavily now—pretty typical for Ireland in January—and she was grateful that he wasn't as speed-hungry in his day-to-day life as he had been on the track. Despite being married to one of the world's smoothest racing drivers, she hadn't been allowed to set foot in any of his supercars. He had all but packed them away in the basement of the Swiss chalet, joking that he would see them again in eighteen years.

He was ridiculously excited about the baby, buying all the newest gadgets and suggesting the most outlandish names he could think of every chance he could get. The idea that they had almost done this separately…it was unthinkable. Making love with Grayson had been life-changing…but being loved by him every day was everything.

They came to a stop at the side of the road and Izzy frowned at the sight of a very deserted, very brunch-less field. 'What exactly are you up to?'

'You'll have to follow me to find out.'

She did, getting her canvas sneakers soaked in the process, which prompted her husband's instant grumbling. Despite his having bought her no fewer than five new pairs of increasingly expensive boots she still insisted on wearing her old favourites from time to time.

'Happy anniversary.' He smiled.

Izzy raised her eyebrows, looking around for some sign of what was going on here. 'It's not our first wedding anniversary for another five months.'

'Not that anniversary.' He offered his elbow, holding her steady as she stepped across the hilly terrain.

'Oh…' she said as realisation dawned. She'd entirely lost track of the weeks since the nausea had stopped and the tiredness had begun. 'Is that today?'

'It is.' Grayson smiled as he stepped behind her, holding her close against his chest. 'Happy Platonic Baby-Making Deal Day.'

She smiled at the warmth of him holding her, and at the reminder of the day that felt like a lifetime ago. The day that had begun with her waking up and thinking that all her perfect plans had been ruined and had ended with her in the arms of the man who would become the closest thing to home she had ever felt.

'Hmm…so how is the whole platonic part going for you?' she asked.

'Best business deal of my life.'

'You know, some people have first date anniversaries…'

'Those people sound very boring. Some people have Paris—we have a Swiss fertility clinic mix-up.'

'You were so frazzled.' She laughed.

'You'd have been frazzled too if you'd just realised you wanted the very thing you'd always said you didn't.' He kissed her again, harder this time. 'And then you came along and ruined all my playboy plans.'

'Oh, I remember strict bachelor Grayson…he was such a cranky man.'

'He was misunderstood,' Grayson chided. 'Not surprising, considering he refers to himself in the third person. Who knew one freak snowstorm was all it would take to change everything.'

'For the better, I hope?'

'The best. And now, with this next chapter coming our way…' He rubbed the soft skin beneath her belly button with tender care. 'I've decided it's time for us both to step out of our comfort zones even more. What do you say, Goldilocks? Are you ready to be brave with me?'

'I know that I'm not the most outdoorsy type, but I don't think I need a pep talk to agree to a picnic.' She smiled—then realised his jaw was ticking again.

'We're not here for a picnic. Have you any idea where we are?'

Izzy looked around again at the rolling green hills, trying to find a landmark. 'Pretty sure we're in a field, babe…'

'It's ten acres of land, waiting for someone to build their dream home on it. Our home, if we go ahead with the sale.' He pulled a rolled-up piece of paper from his jacket pocket, smoothing it out. 'This is just a blueprint. I've told the architect that you'll have the final say…'

Izzy looked at the blueprint and felt her throat tighten painfully. It was a house. Her house. The one she'd told him about on what she'd thought was their last snowy night together a lifetime ago. As a child she'd drawn that square-fronted homestead over and over again, like a mantra, dreaming that one day she might actually get to stay in one place. He'd remembered it all. Every detail. Even the red front door.

She closed her eyes, her fragile hormones not strong enough to withstand the wave of emotion that swept through her, crumpling her face as the tears began to fall. But she didn't hold in her tears—not with Grayson. She let them out freely, burying her face in the safety of her husband's warm neck as she processed the beauty of his plans for their future.

For a while Grayson was powerless to do anything but stand still and shelter Isabel's sobbing form in his arms. He'd spent the past two months sourcing the perfect location for them to lay down roots, while also reorganising his greatly reduced schedule for the following year. But still he knew how sensitive his wife was about the possibility of leaving her first home— the one she had found and fixed up and made her own against all the odds.

He'd prepared himself to allow her whatever reaction came naturally, but seeing her so visibly undone tightened the ever-present knot that had taken hold of his lungs.

'I'm sorry for the tears...' Her voice was barely more than a whisper, her cheek still firmly buried in the layers of his coat as she hiccuped between words.

'Don't apologise, my love. You don't have to say anything at all if it's too much.'

She inhaled a deep breath and sighed, but it wasn't

until she lightly thumped her fist against his chest and began to chuckle at her own emotional outburst that he felt the tight bands release his chest.

He framed Isabel's face in his hands, wiping away the last of her tears as she smiled up at him. 'I know we can make our home anywhere,' he said softly. 'But if we want to get serious about our other plans for the future I thought we should get started on settling in a home that would better suit a growing family.'

The little two-bedroom cottage she'd bought had been the perfect part-time home base over the past year, as they'd split their time between Ireland and Grayson's international travel schedule. And it was a perfect size for their soon-to-be family of three. But they had recently decided that adoption was something they both wanted to do too, when the time was right.

'This place is the size of a small county.' She chuckled. 'Exactly how many children are you planning for us to have?'

'As many as you'll let me.' He smirked.

'Let's just focus on this one for now.' She laid one hand across her stomach, cradling the place where their child grew steadily.

'As far as gifts go…is it too much?' he asked.

'It's *entirely* too much, and I absolutely love it,' she said, reaching up on tiptoe to press her lips to his jaw. 'I love you, no matter where we live. But building our own home together here and filling it with love…it's my dream come true.'

'*You* are my dream come true, Isabel O' Sullivan.'

She grinned, her cheeks turning a bright rosy pink. 'You need to stop saying these things. I'm already one step away from climbing you like a tree at every moment.'

'Well, we *are* in a field.' Grayson moved his lips along the soft shell of her ear, his voice a sultry whisper. 'How about I stand very still and you show off those climbing skills?'

'I was hoping you'd say that.'

No matter how many times he kissed this beautiful woman, every time felt just as explosive and all-consuming as the first. Her hands wrapped around his neck, scorching his skin and holding him close as she commanded and demanded from him. He gathered the firm, luscious swells of her behind in his hands and pulled her up against the hard ridge of his erection, growling when she moaned into his mouth.

He was vaguely aware that they were in a muddy field, and that it had begun to drizzle with rain again, but for once he was too happy to care about the details. Their kiss was one of pure need, filled with joy and passion for the life they were creating together, both inside and all around them. Desire vibrated along his nerve-endings, igniting the passion that never seemed too far away when they were together, and spurring him on to claim her body completely in the way he knew best.

But then the wind stilled for a brief moment, allowing just enough silence for the low, growling protest of Isabel's stomach to be heard.

'I think your climbing will have to wait until after

brunch.' He smirked, letting out a full laugh at the resulting pout that transformed her kiss-swollen lips.

'Okay, but promise me we'll come back.'

'We're going to be here quite a lot, I'd imagine. As I'm self-appointed project manager. I can't guarantee it will be ready before the baby arrives…but I think I'm going to enjoy the challenge of trying.'

They walked hand in hand back across the rolling green landscape that was to become their family home, and Grayson felt peace wash over him with every tiny drop of rain that landed upon his skin. He loved the temperamental Irish weather just as much as he loved his chaotic wife and the way she never did anything he expected.

'Are you seriously going to try to build an entire house in six months?' she asked, chewing on her lower lip. 'Is that not quite fast?'

'Darling, most of our relationship has been fast.'

'I wouldn't change a thing about our fast track to happy-ever-after,' she said, and smiled, twirling into his arms for another kiss.

* * * * *

If you were head over heels for
The Bump in Their Forbidden Reunion
then look out for the next instalment in
The Fast Track Billionaires Club trilogy,
coming soon!

And while you wait, why not dive straight
into these other stories
by Amanda Cinelli?

Returning to Claim His Heir
Stolen in Her Wedding Gown
The Billionaire's Last-Minute Marriage
Pregnant in the Italian's Palazzo
A Ring to Claim Her Crown

Available now!

#4177 CINDERELLA'S ONE-NIGHT BABY
by Michelle Smart

A glamorous evening at the palace with Spanish tycoon Andrés? Irresistible! Even if Gabrielle knows this one encounter is all the guarded Spaniard will allow himself. Yet, when the chemistry simmering between them erupts into mind-blowing passion, the nine-month consequence will tie her and Andrés together forever...

#4178 HIDDEN HEIR WITH HIS HOUSEKEEPER
A Diamond in the Rough
by Heidi Rice

Self-made billionaire Mason Foxx would never forget the sizzling encounter he had with society princess Bea Medford. But his empire comes first, always. Until months later, he gets the ultimate shock: Bea isn't just the housekeeper at the hotel he's staying at—she's also carrying his child!

#4179 THE SICILIAN'S DEAL FOR "I DO"
Brooding Billionaire Brothers
by Clare Connelly

Marriage offered Mia Marini distance from her oppressive family, so Luca Cavallaro's desertion of their convenient wedding devastated her, especially after their mind-blowing kiss! Then Luca returns with a scandalous proposition: risk it all for a no-strings week together...and claim the wedding night they never had!

#4180 PREGNANCY CLAUSE IN THEIR PAPER MARRIAGE
by Kate Hewitt

Honoring the strict rules of his on-paper marriage, Christos Diakis has fought hard to ignore the electricity simmering between him and his wife, Lana. Her request that they have a baby rocks the very foundations of their union. And Christos has neither the power—nor wish—to decline...

HPCNMRA0124

#4181 THE FORBIDDEN BRIDE HE STOLE
by Millie Adams

Hannah will do *anything* to avoid the magnetic pull of her guardian, Apollo, including marry another. Then Apollo shockingly steals her from the altar, and a dangerous flame is ignited. Hannah must decide—is their passion a firestorm she can survive unscathed, or will it burn everything down?

#4182 AWAKENED IN HER ENEMY'S PALAZZO
by Kim Lawrence

Grace Stewart never expected to inherit a palazzo from her beloved late employer. Or that his ruthless tech mogul son, Theo Ranieri, would move in until she agrees to sell! Sleeping under the same roof fuels their agonizing attraction. There's just one place their standoff can end—in Theo's bed!

#4183 THE KING SHE SHOULDN'T CRAVE
by Lela May Wight

Promoted from spare to heir after tragedy struck, Angelo can't be distracted from his duty. Being married to the woman he has always craved—his brother's intended queen—has him on the precipice of self-destruction. The last thing he needs is for Natalia to recognize their dangerous attraction. If she does, there's nothing to stop it from becoming all-consuming...

#4184 UNTOUCHED UNTIL THE GREEK'S RETURN
by Susan Stephens

Innocent Rosy Bloom came to Greece looking for peace. But there's nothing peaceful about the storm of desire tycoon Xander Tsakis unleashes in her upon his return to his island home! Anything they share would be temporary, but Xander's dangerously thrilling proximity has cautious Rosy abandoning all reason!

HPCNMRB0124

Get 3 FREE REWARDS!

We'll send you 2 FREE Books <u>plus</u> a FREE Mystery Gift.

PRESENTS
His Innocent for One Spanish Night
CAROL MARINELLI

PRESENTS
Bound by the Italian's "I Do"
MICHELLE SMART

FREE Value Over **$20**

Both the **Harlequin® Desire** and **Harlequin Presents®** series feature compelling novels filled with passion, sensuality and intriguing scandals.